# THE
# PLEASURE DIAL

An Erotocomedic Novel of Old-Time Radio

By

JEREMY EDWARDS

*The Pleasure Dial: An Erotocomedic Novel of Old-Time Radio*
Copyright © 2011 by Jeremy Edwards

Published by 1001 Nights Press 2013
First published in 2011 by OC Press
Cover design by CoverDomme
Book design by BookDomme

Printed in the United States

ISBN-10: 061578187X

ISBN-13: 978-0615781877

# Acknowledgements

The author wishes to broadcast his coast-to-coast appreciation of OC Press for getting *The Pleasure Dial* on the air, and of 1001 Nights Press for keeping it on the air.

# Dedication

*For Helia Brookes, with all my love.*

# Table of Contents

# Prologue

Artie was looking up the skirt of his favorite Macy's mannequin when he decided to head for the West Coast. Her name was Trixie (Artie had decided), and he could always count on her to listen patiently while he tried out new material. It certainly beat telling jokes to thin air. Moreover, he'd found that gazing at the sleek, impressionistic bareness beneath her skirt of the week – Trixie never wore lingerie – gave him the serenity he needed to make important decisions.

Yes, he determined in that moment – crouching on the sidewalk, the strain on his muscles a small price to pay for the view – that he would take the job writing for Sid Heffy. Trixie's mannequin heinie seemed to smile approval.

After wandering around New York for a couple of years with his talent tied to his finger like a balloon, Artie Plask had hit that first lucky break on which he'd built a career. Now, in his late twenties, he was so busy writing bits for burlesque comics and gossip columnists and advertising men that he had the luxury of sending the spillover work to worthy friends who were still establishing themselves.

He'd been thinking of moving into radio full-time for a while – he'd had a parade of offers, and the fill-in spots he'd consented to had been some of the most stimulating work he'd ever done. Radio kept you on your toes, forced you to be as brilliant as you could be. The business was expanding, despite the Depression, and the requirements of creating so many fresh shows every week for a coast-to-coast audience meant that a joke writer with a good reputation could have his pick of jobs.

But Heffy was the first radio star who had tried to lure Artie to California. That made the prospect of radio seem not merely like a new gig, but like a new life.

Looking at Trixie – at her unblinking yet sympathetic blue eyes, now that he'd risen from his voyeuristic crouch – Artie admitted that he liked the idea of a new life, content as he was here in New York.

He blew the skirted statue a kiss before walking off toward Western Union to answer the wire from the Heffy people.

# Chapter 1

"You mean I'm supposed to report to Mr. Heffy's *house?*"
"Welcome to Hollywood, kid," answered Sid's head writer, and the telephone earpiece seemed to bristle in Artie's hand with the force of Mickey's nasal vibrato. "Oh, and stop by the five-and-dime and get yourself some swim trunks. Sometimes we work by the pool."

"Sid likes that, huh?"

"His daughter does."

Artie knew he could work anywhere, having written gags on streetcars, at the Y, even during slow-moving portions of his cousins' bar mitzvahs. Still, he'd assumed that the writing team of *Dressinger Clothing Presents the Sid Heffy Show* would be working in an office somewhere downtown, like the radio writers did back in New York.

He liked children, but he hoped Heffy's daughter wouldn't be too disruptive. He didn't relish the prospect of getting splashed by some eight-year-old's aquatic gymnastics just when the next punch line was firing through his brain.

Showing up for his first day on the job with a notebook and a pair of trunks made Artie feel like the taxi ride had landed him back in summer camp – and the summery spring weather of Los Angeles added to the illusion. Coming from a world where one went into an office, rain, sleet, or shine, and worked, he told himself he'd have to adjust to this world where you showed up in the sunshine at your boss's mansion, as if for a lawn party … and worked.

"Whaddya want?"

"How do you do, Mr. Heffy. I'm Artie Plask, your new writer."

The man opened the front door wide enough to let Artie through, all the while rolling his eyes for the benefit of an imaginary audience. "So this schmuck from back east thinks I'm Sid Heffy."

Nobody had warned Artie that the star employed a majordomo who looked – and acted – very much like the star himself, whom Artie had seen many a time in the movies. He reflected that the hiring choice showed a peculiar flavor of vanity on Heffy's part.

"I beg your pardon, Mr. – "

"Lubb." He sighed it out, as though the syllable itself ought to convey every detail of the crap he had to put up with in this job – such as opening the door to schmucks from back east.

Sid Heffy (like his double, Lubb) was a slightly rotund gentleman whose egg-shaped head and downy blond hair could not help but suggest, in one way or another, something newly hatched. Large, gaping eyes and a small, tight mouth conspired to evoke suspicious befuddlement – the basis of Heffy's act, even in the invisible medium of radio, and, from the comedy writer's point of view, the foundation for every line handed to him. And though no one was writing for Lubb, Artie had already noted that the man's mimicry of his boss extended beyond what Nature had arranged, into the realm of demeanor. Having met this mimeograph first, he couldn't help feeling that his first-day introduction to Sid himself would be anticlimactic.

This concern proved moot, however, as Sid Heffy was not in.

"But go on through," instructed Lubb, in a tone implying he would have preferred to tell Artie to get lost. "The other writers are back there on the patio, and Elyse is keeping the jerks company."

"Elyse?"

"Elyse. Elyse *Heffernan*." Again the butler rolled his eyes. "Sid's daughter."

Artie, who hadn't even remembered that "Heffy" was a stage name, and who also hadn't spent his train journey boning up on the dramatis personae of his new employer's family, felt as stupid as Lubb intended him to feel, and this was quickly putting him into a funk. Maybe the presence of an eight-year-old would be welcome, after all, to brighten the mood.

But there was no eight-year-old on the patio.

Instead, there was a breathtakingly picturesque woman of perhaps twenty-two or twenty-three. She was seated at the edge of the pool, completely naked. The downy blond hair that ran in her family was visible in two locations, and tickled Artie's eyeballs from both of them.

He observed that the skinny young men who dotted the poolside landscape in their patio chairs were giving the beauty only fragments of their attention. Clearly acclimated to these working conditions, the fellows seemed fairly absorbed in their notepads and the rapidly expanding volume of material emanating from the typewriter.

Mickey, who was at the Olivetti helm, was on a roll, and Artie knew that you didn't interrupt a writer in flow. So he stood at the edge of the patio smiling at Miss Heffernan, waiting patiently for Mickey to take a breath and discover his arrival. It was scarcely a hardship.

Elyse had evidently been in the water some time earlier, and her nipples still glistened in the morning light. She held Artie's gaze, looking friendly, clever, and a tad hungry for attention. After thirty seconds of this paradisial stalemate she beckoned him poolward; he was about to accept the unspoken invitation when Mickey's nasal tone broke in on the idyll.

"Oh good, Plask is here. Pull up a chair, Artie."

Elyse shrugged and stood up, and he watched the arced lines of her bottom as she plunged headfirst into the water.

Mickey introduced him to the other seven "boys." Artie shook hands, memorized names, then looked around.

"You said I was being added as a tenth writer, didn't you? So if I'm the tenth man, where's the ninth man?"

"Right here at home plate."

The voice, though only moderately high in pitch, was unmistakably female – and it had not come from the direction of the pool, where Elyse was busy doing laps. No, this voice came from the doorway back into the house, a doorway that Artie was certain had been empty a moment earlier.

She was a compactly built woman about his age, svelte and lively looking, who was dressed in subdued tones that emphasized the acuity in her face. She immediately reminded Artie of every witty woman he'd known in New York, with all the ones he'd never encountered piled in for good measure.

For some reason, she was carrying an enormous quill pen.

"You don't write radio scripts with that thing, do you?" Artie blurted. Writers did have eccentric habits – though not by comparison with the on-air personalities.

She strode toward him jauntily, like the more elegant type of European stage clown, and Artie admired the way her theatricality electrified every inch of her petite frame.

"Don't you think we should be properly introduced before I tell you what I do or don't do with my feather? Mariel Fenton." She extended her hand amiably.

Her black-coffee eyes were birdlike in their attentiveness, only warmer, and Artie had the feeling that anything he said to Mariel, or even near Mariel, would be processed with intelligence and compassion – and never taken more seriously than was warranted.

"I'm Artie Plask."

"I know," she confessed. "I just wanted to hear you say it."

He laughed. "I'm glad you're so easy to accommodate."

"I'm easy to lotsofthings." Having tossed off the line,

she efficiently deposited her quill in the band of her gray cloche hat, clapped her hands together, and addressed the group: "So, boys, what's the story?"

Mickey grabbed three typewritten pages and handed them to her. Mariel quickly scanned them.

"No offense, boys, but this..."

"Stinks?" a writer named Gabe offered helpfully.

Mariel turned to Artie. "It is to be noted that I never actually employ that word here." She addressed the group again. "Oh, well, let's see what we can salvage." She found her way to a vacant chair.

"Is she your most senior writer?" Artie whispered to Mickey.

"Nah – she's just the smartest."

"Look at this: first page," said Mariel. "Heffy says he's brewing some tea. There is absolutely nothing funny about brewing tea, Mickey."

"It's only an incidental line," said a writer named Howard.

"*Nothing* is incidental in good comedy," Mariel retorted. "Heffy should say he's boiling an egg. Now *that's* amusing – though offhand I couldn't say why."

"I think it's partly because Heffy looks like an egg," said Artie. Mariel's approach to scriptwriting was very much in line with his own philosophy, and he hoped she'd approve of his insight.

She did. "*Yes*," she said, with a decisive nod.

The work was intense and productive over the hours that followed. At lunchtime, he saw Elyse wrap her glittering form in a towel and glide into the house. She returned an hour later, clothed this time, clutching a monograph on modern art. Every now and then her laughter redounded musically across the tiles, obviously not provoked by Miró and Kandinsky, but by a stray joke that fell sweetly on her ears as the writers tossed ideas around the patio.

"Good work, Artie," said Mickey, when it was time to quit. Three of Artie's jokes had actually made it into the working script, which meant he stood a good chance of seeing one line make it onto the air Saturday night. For his first session, he knew this *was* good work.

Mariel had written about half the show, including most of the best lines. She stalked the patio when brainstorming, waving her feather like a zany orchestra conductor while Mickey scrambled to keep pace with her on the typewriter. Her buttock muscles flexed beautifully beneath her dark skirt as she strode to and fro, and her bosom bounced with sober confidence.

When the session broke up, Mariel stretched like a cat, and she smiled at Artie. He rose from his chair so that she could get by him on her way out. But instead of leaving, she walked toward the pool, where Elyse was lounging in a deck chair.

"How are you today, Elyse?"

"Wonderful, thanks," she answered breathily yet melodically, rising from the lounger. "You?"

"I'm swell. We showed that script a thing or two, and your old man's funniness will thus remain intact."

Heffy's daughter grinned broadly. "Thank you for keeping Daddy funny." Her tone dropped to a conspiratorial hush. "He thinks he's really a great actor, doesn't he?"

"Indeed he does – and that's part of what's so funny about him. Say, have you met Artie, the new kid?"

Artie stepped forward. "I saw a lot of Elyse earlier," he explained to Mariel. "But I guess I didn't get a chance to introduce myself," he said to Elyse apologetically.

"I knew you'd want to meet him," said Mariel cryptically.

"Yes," said Elyse, looking at him with sparkling green eyes. "I adore Daddy's writers." She surprised Artie by touching his chest. "Well, I'm off to my boudoir." She laughed colorfully, as if treasuring a magical secret, then walked gracefully into the house. Even dressed, Elyse somehow looked nude to Artie.

The other writers had long departed, and Elyse's exit

left Mariel and Artie in a poolside tête-à-tête.

"You do understand she's expecting you to join her there, yes?" Mariel asked.

"What?"

"Elyse likes to try out all the writers, at least once apiece."

He felt his right eyebrow clicking itself upward. "I see. Well, I've certainly heard of less agreeable conditions of employment."

"Oh, goodness, it's nothing like a 'condition of employment.' Elyse is merely a pansexual sensualist looking for some innocent kicks. We all think of her as a sort of freelance sex goddess. But it sure results in a lot of loyalty among Heffy's staff. Don't forget, you're an addition, not a replacement. Of course, Sid no doubt attributes the low turnover to his own charisma."

"Yes, I imagine he would." Though Artie had yet to meet Heffy, the star's reputation for self-infatuation preceded him. Nor had it been diminished by the presence of the "made in his own image" butler.

"No, participation in Elyse's little program is not compulsory. Benny declined," Mariel noted, pointing to the chair that writer had occupied during the script session. "He's known to prefer the company of men."

"But she's taken all the rest of them to bed?"

"Most of them. A couple of the boys are working from monogamous scripts. I'm afraid that Hollywood isn't entirely what you fantasize it is – you know, one big orgy."

"Hey," Artie protested, "you've got the wrong guy. Or at least the wrong fantasy."

"Oh, yeah?"

"I didn't come here looking for one big orgy. I'll be perfectly content with a series of smaller orgies."

She laughed appreciatively. "I apologize for misreading you."

He bowed his head graciously.

"You said our local goddess was 'pansexual.' I've never

heard that word before, but I know my Latin prefixes."

"It's Greek. The prefix, I mean."

"Oh. Right. So tell me: did you decline to participate in the Elyse program as well?"

Mariel half winked, half shrugged. "Me? You know me ..."

"No, I really don't know you," he grinned. "But I have a feeling this is something I ought to redress."

"Exactly – and as soon as you're redressed, we'll take steps in that direction. But first things first." She prodded him between the ribs. "Elyse's boudoir is on the second floor, opposite the stairs. Unless you're going to disappoint the poor girl."

"Me? You know me ..."

# Chapter 2

A few minutes later, Artie crept into Elyse's boudoir. He thought the room might be better termed a *den*. His eyes roamed from beaded curtain to extravagant ottoman, from incense candles to luxurious bedclothes, and then to the sprawling, half-naked woman positioned upon them, gyrating with lust and caressing her own flesh with a corner of silk sheet.

"Funny – I thought Mariel said you were a sensualist." It was Artie's nature, not to mention his job, to open with a joke.

"Come here, sweet Artie Plask."

He closed the door behind him but then hesitated, humbled by her apparent proficiency. "Are you sure you need me? You seem to be doing all right by yourself."

"I may not *need* you, strictly speaking ... but I want you."

"Fair enough."

"Yes, you look like you'd be able to please a woman. *This* woman, at any rate."

Artie was grateful for whatever it was about him – his sympathetic eyes? his playful mouth? – that evidently advertised his devotion to female pleasure to those looking to obtain some. He approached the bedside, trying to absorb the testosterone-thrilling reality that the divine Elyse was going to crack her fruit for him, to show him her juice.

"Mariel's right. You *are* a goddess, and I can't imagine a lovelier one."

"Thank you," she purred. "Daddy thinks I could be a movie star."

"But that would mean getting dressed."

"Exactly."

"You're pretty happy hanging around here, aren't you?"

"Yes. I love witty men," she confessed in a drawn-out moan. "And women. And I'm the luckiest girl in the world, because the wittiest people in Hollywood come to my house every day and make me wet from morning to night."

"On Tuesday and Thursday nights, you mean." According to Mickey, those were the only evenings the team worked late.

"I bet the entire swimming pool smells like my horny pussy," Elyse declared proudly, looking Artie in the eye.

He lowered his ass to the edge of the bed, his hard-on wrestling his thigh for top billing.

"Your jokes made me laugh today," she continued.

This was his kind of foreplay. "Which one did you like best?"

"The one about ignoring." She tittered at the memory.

*There's a customer waiting, and I don't want to ignore him. I don't want to... but I'd like to.* Yes, that would work well in Heffy's voice. "Thank you. That's a subtle one."

"I love that word, don't you? *Subtle.* It sounds like a softly licking tongue."

Artie knew a song cue when he heard one. He pulled the sheet away from her body, and focused his attention on the sex-damp blond fur he'd thereby revealed.

The *ohhhh-oh* she voiced when he ran a finger along the seam of her lips made her sound pleasantly surprised by his touch – though the "surprise" component was clearly an illusion. She shifted her hips to welcome him, and he kissed the sticky sweetness of her moist curls to continue the corporeal dialogue.

When he took hold of her bottom cheeks, their softness *was* a surprise; where they'd appeared shapely but firm while in action at the pool, in the bedroom they seemed to have undergone a metamorphosis from shapely muscles into equally shapely pillows.

He licked the length of her opening, and Elyse *ohhhhh*'d again. She gaped for him, and her clit sparkled like a swollen jewel in some undersea treasure chest. He continued licking.

Her buttocks slapped themselves against his palms, anticipating his caresses. "Keep licking. Ohhhhh ... Lick my pussy all night." She squeezed his frame between her knees, and the fragrance of her arousal cloaked him as he dined on her.

"You tickle so nicely," she moaned, churning her sex in his face. "My mind, my pussy ... you funny men tickle me everywhere."

In that spirit, Artie slipped a finger up the crack of her ass.

"Oh, god, yes, tickle me there, too. Everywhere, every –" She broke off into sensualistic giggles.

He deepened the trajectory of his tongue, making sure to lavish sensation on every bit of pleasure-loving cunt flesh he could reach. Elyse writhed in slow motion, giggling and whimpering *yes*es and *oh god*s, and sponging Artie's muzzle with her juices.

"Oh, go-o-o-o-odddddddd!" She laughed it; cried it; even kicked it, tangling the sheets.

Her clit hovered in his mouth like a gumdrop until, unable to come any more, she lifted him by the shoulders and kissed the top of his head. He turned his face upward, and she devoured his mouth with the abandoned kisses of a woman wallowing in satisfaction.

So this was life on *The Sid Heffy Show*.

Though his erection was raging, Artie felt strangely satisfied too. He'd licked the pussy of a sex goddess until she cried with ecstasy – what more did he want from day one on the job?

But Elyse was not only a goddess, she was a giver; and soon Artie's cock was throbbing excitedly in her fist, his trousers and shorts clutched in her other hand. Her delicious touch was almost so light as to not be there: it felt as if the air itself were giving him the seamless hand job, teasing him quickly and exquisitely to the point of no return. Right before he shot, Elyse kissed his tip, and when he spurted she laughed with delight.

She offered him a nipple to kiss before leaving him to recuperate in her bed. "I'm going for a swim," she said.

Her ass-cheeks, receding through the boudoir door, were still flushed with pleasure.

Artie luxuriated in Elyse's erotic nest for only a moment before the door opened again. He lifted his head to see, not a nude Elyse returning for a towel, but a fully clothed Mariel.

"Hello, Artie." She gave a perfunctory glance at his flaccid cock, as if feeling that this was the polite thing to do. "I thought I should tell you that we've all been fired."

"What?"

"I know – isn't it fun?"

# Chapter 3

It was, perhaps, simply out of shock that Artie neglected to pull his trousers up as Mariel came to sit on the edge of the bed. Whatever the reason, the result was that his cock nestled unobtrusively but quite visibly in his groin while he listened to her reassuring words.

"Now, don't worry, this sort of thing happens all the time around here."

"Mariel Fenton barging into boudoirs?"

"Sid Heffy firing his writers."

"But you said there was low turnover!"

"Precisely – and that's why you shouldn't worry. We're always getting fired, but no one ever actually has to leave. It's only a gesture on Sid's part."

"A *gesture*," Artie snorted. "How thoughtful of him."

"Well, be reasonable. He has to do something once in a while to feel important."

"I didn't even think he was here today."

"Oh, he's here, all right – pretty as a picture, and twice as ugly. He returned ten minutes ago and fired us five minutes ago. Sid is very efficient when he wants to be."

"The guy sounds like a one-man bureaucracy. Say, why were *you* still on the premises?"

She looked away, toward an art nouveau tapestry heavy with libertines – the first trace of self-consciousness he'd seen in her. "I was kind of sticking around to see how everything ... played out." Her confident manner – and her direct gaze – immediately returned; she settled the latter on Artie's sated dick.

"I can't believe I've been fired. I haven't even met the boss."

"*We've* been fired," she said evenly, still studying his anatomy. "Don't be a hot dog. Oh! Sorry, that was an indelicate choice of words under the circumstances. I didn't ..."

But they were both laughing too hard for her to finish disclaiming the remark. Something very comfortable seemed to fill the room – something that was also intoxicating, as if the laughter were laughing *gas* – and it felt perfectly natural when Mariel collapsed on his convulsing shoulders and stifled her warm guffaws in the hollow of his throat.

Where Elyse's laughter had a celestial magic – even when carnally provoked – Mariel's had a solid presence. It seemed to resonate in Artie's bones.

"Fine," she said at last. "Go ahead and be a hot dog. It suits you."

They let the laughter linger between them for a minute.

"Now, then. Pull your pants up." Swift as lightning, she yanked the oversized feather from her cloche and gave his scrotum a quick brush.

He squealed gleefully. Then he glanced at the untelescoping sausage in his lap, drawing her line of sight back to it with his own.

"I can't help noticing, Miss Fenton, that your words and your actions appear to be at cross purposes."

"Sorry – I couldn't resist. I've wanted to tickle your balls ever since I first barged into the room. As you are no doubt aware, women of my intelligence are subject to a large array of sensible impulses, such as tickling a friend's balls with a feather. Bearing this in mind, I hope you appreciate my vast reserves of self-control."

"At the moment, I think I'd appreciate them more in absentia."

She hesitated an instant before giving him a kiss on the cheek.

"Now, come on, pants up. Heffy wants us out of here, for the time being. We must humor the old golf ball, until he changes his mind."

They shared a cab back to central Hollywood, arriving at the courtyard of Artie's apartment first.

"So, what do I do in the morning?"

"I don't know. What do you usually do in the morning?"

"I only got here two days ago. I don't 'usually' do anything yet."

"Ah, a *tabula rasa* – a clean slate."

"I *know* what a *tabula rasa* is. I think I'll even be correct this time when I identify it as Latin."

"Just think: we can mold you, shape you, turn you into the ideal man."

"You're implying that I'm not already the ideal man? I'm terribly hurt, Dr. Frankenstein. But getting back to tomorrow morning ... what I was trying to get at is the question of what I do regarding my status with the Sid Heffy organization."

"Oh, that. Personally, I'm planning to phone Mickey first thing."

"All right. I'll do the same. In fact, I think until I get my bearings I'll just do whatever you do."

"Okay, but that will involve sitting down when you pee."

"You may need to demonstrate that one for me."

"I shall look forward to it. See you tomorrow, Artie."

"Yes – *if* Heffy ..."

"Nonsense. I told you not to worry."

"G'morning, Mickey. Plask here. I heard a little rumor that we've been fired."

"What the hell are you chuckling about?"

"Sorry. I was advised not to take it too seriously."

"I'm afraid this time is different, kid."

"Uh-oh. Sid is that annoyed with us, huh?"

"No, it's worse than that. He's not annoyed with us at all," said Mickey.

"I don't understand."

"It's nothing to do with us. It's just that Sid Heffy has decided to turn his show into a goddamn radio *drama*. Effective immediately."

"What?"

"I was at the house at seven o'clock this morning, and Sid was on the phone with some hound-faced playhouse type. I gather the bastard is all set to remake him as radio's answer to Hedda Gabbler."

Artie wondered if Mickey could really be sure the playhouse type was hound-faced just from hearing Sid talk to him on the phone. For that matter, it puzzled him that any self-respecting playwright – hound-faced or otherwise – would be awake at 7 a.m.

"I tell you, Artie, I always thought Sid's dramatic delusions were a harmless trademark that added something to his persona. If I'd known the jerk was going to *act* on them, then ..."

"Then what?"

He could virtually hear Mickey's shrug over the phone. "Then I would have known, I guess."

"Well, maybe it won't pan out, eh?"

"Yeah, maybe. That's what Mariel said."

It made Artie absurdly proud to learn that he'd reacted the same way she had. "That reminds me – how do I get in touch with Mariel?"

"You turn around." The voice came from the apartment doorway.

"Never mind, Mickey." Artie hung up the phone.

"This is a regular part of your routine, isn't it?" he said to his visitor.

"Everyone has their shtick. And you can't deny it's convenient to have me materialize whenever you need me."

"True. It's undeniably convenient ... if a bit disorienting."

"You'll get used to it."

"I look forward to that."

He rose from his seat, and Mariel automatically took his place at the tiny desk, spinning the chair around to face the room. "I just thought that while we were out of work I'd drop in on you, to break up the monotony around here with my own brand of monotony."

"Your company certainly isn't monotonous yet," he said gallantly – and truthfully.

He began to pace. "Look, this isn't so bad, right? We can all get jobs on other shows in a trice." He snapped his fingers.

"That was a *snap*, not a trice. But it's true – none of us will be jobless for long."

"Still, it would be a shame to see the old gang break up."

Mariel laughed. "The 'old gang'? You've only been with us for one day."

"It was a very productive day. And a very enjoyable one."

"Speaking of Elyse, I have her private motor car outside."

"Complete with chauffeur?"

"No chauffeur. Elyse drives."

"When does she find the time?"

"Well, that's why she lets me borrow it whenever I want. It's just a two-seater, though really you can fit three if you squeeze." She made a slightly lewd gesture to illustrate the concept of *squeezing*, which Artie found unnecessary but pleasant.

"Open car or closed?" he asked.

"Closed. Why?"

"I was just wondering if it smells like ... the swimming pool."

"Say, I hope you don't have some silly idea that you're going to settle down with Elyse in a bungalow."

"Pfft. Trick a girl like that into giving up a life like this? Even if I could – which I sincerely doubt – I wouldn't."

Mariel smiled warmly. "I like the way you think, Plask."

"So ... am I the only one who *wasn't* at the Heffernan mansion at seven o'clock this morning?"

"No, the rest of the boys are presumably still in their footsie pajamas. Mickey was the only one welcome, and very temporarily at that. I had to pretend I was there to borrow Elyse's car – she wasn't awake yet, but Lubb gave me the keys. It will come in handy, though."

"For what?"

"I haven't decided yet."

"You have a delightful way of putting the horseless carriage before the horse."

"Glad to oblige. Oh, I know!" She bounced out of the chair. "Let's drive over to Culver City."

"Okay. But what's in Culver City?"

"Lila and Henry."

# Chapter 4

Mariel waved at the studio security guard as she steered the little auto into the gargantuan lot.

"Good morning, Charles. Lila Lowell is expecting me."

"Lila *Lowell*?" goggled Artie, as the gatekeeper cheerfully waved them through. Lila was one of the biggest stars, a household name even among those who hadn't actually seen any of her steamy movies.

"Naturally, Lila Lowell. How many people named Lila do you imagine we have in this town?"

"And she's expecting you."

"Yes, in a blanket kind of way: she knows I could drop by the soundstage at any time. I used to write her publicity, and she's never managed to fully extricate herself from my society."

"I see. And what manner of household name, then, is this Henry?"

"Henry is Lila's personal costume and makeup specialist. A real artist. So if Lila's playing a vamp, for instance, she turns to Henry every time her makeup fades and she needs to be *re*vamped. Lila won't do so much as throw a brassiere over her tits without consulting him."

The car went quiet while an image of the sultry screen idol parading topless in a dressing room, waiting for her Henry, hovered in Artie's mind – and his crotch.

"What are you thinking about, Artie?"

"I believe you know damn well what I'm thinking about."

Mariel chuckled as she pulled into a parking space.

"Well, here we are. But speaking of makeup, let me just fix mine before we go in. This will also give the gentleman a moment to adjust his penis before he has to stand up and exit the car."

"You think of everything."

"Almost everything. I should have brought a change of panties, since apparently you're going to be entertaining me with hard-ons all over the place."

"As a matter of fact, they're always in the same place."

"Oh, I bet we can find somewhere new to put them."

No sooner had they been admitted to the set than the director began a take.

The Lila Lowell scene being staged was instantly reminiscent of every Lila Lowell scene Artie had viewed through a haze of popcorn in midtown Manhattan. Lila, dressed in a black "negligee" that most women would be proud to wear in the ballroom, reclined on a day bed, looking simultaneously fascinated and bored by the tuxedo-clad lover who sat beside her – a dual impression that few thespians could convey.

Though the man was ostensibly wooing her, most of the dialogue was Lila's. Her lips, moodily sensuous in black lipstick, uttered line after line of existentially erotic observations in a voice that resonated with charisma and even "heart," despite its languidness. Finally, having worked herself into a blasé sort of passion, Lila seized her co-star and kissed him fervently until the director cut.

As the crew scurried around preparing for the next scene, Mariel waved to her friend. Lila smiled in recognition and began making her way toward them.

"Hello, dear," the star said almost inaudibly when she arrived at Mariel's side. Her bearing was surprisingly timid, her speech and movements small and inhibited – a dramatic contrast with her self-possessed, magnetic screen persona.

"Lila, this is Artie."

Lila smiled faintly. Her eyes wouldn't meet his.

"I'm sure you'll warm up to him right away," Mariel added. "He's a good egg, not to mention a top-notch gag writer and a rather yummy male individual – for those of us with a taste for male individuals."

"Take your picture?" Lila whispered to Artie.

"Huh? Sure, okay." He turned a puzzled face to Mariel, while Miss Lowell retrieved a Brownie from a nearby table.

"She takes everyone," Mariel explained in a discreet undertone. "It helps her break the ice."

When Lila returned with the camera, Artie gave her his biggest ice-breaking grin.

"Hey, you haven't smiled that big for *me*," said Mariel.

"*You* didn't take my picture," he shrugged.

"Don't have a camera," said Mariel. "Surely, that's not the only way?"

He was just reaching into his heart for the next serving of innuendo when the director called, "Places!"

Mariel grabbed the star by her shoulder. "Lila, before you leave: How would you go about convincing Sid Heffy that he isn't cut out for serious drama?"

Artie noticed the delicately arched eyebrow that accompanied Lila's reply. "Direct him to a mirror?" she whispered.

"No, he already spends most of his time in front of one." Mariel turned to Artie. "I bet that's why he wasn't at the house yesterday – he probably found a hotel lobby with an even larger mirror than the one in his bedroom."

Lila laughed silently, then waved her fingers in a goodbye and headed back to the set.

After the experience of conversing with Lila, Artie was startled by the loud, confident clarity of her voice when she once again went before the cameras. He saw that she was now playing to a different beau – though apart from mustache style, the two gentlemen seemed fairly interchangeable.

*"There's a void in my soul, Hubert,"* she intoned, gesturing toward the very bottom of her abdomen on the word *soul. "A void as empty as your head. Come, why don't you marry me? It'll*

*be the grandest month you ever had, and we'll be through in time for the season at Monte Carlo."*

"Ready?" Mariel whispered.

"No. I haven't seen this picture before."

"We should find Henry while Lila isn't using him."

Mariel led him to the exit, and, as soon as the shot was completed, they *creeeeeak*-ed open the door and stepped into the major-motion-picture-studio sunlight.

"Stick close to me," she said. "Otherwise you'll be lost in this high-rent rabbit warren before you know it, and we'll all wonder what ever became of you – until you unwittingly show up in the chorus of some B movie we're about to walk out on."

Though his legs were considerably longer than hers, he was surprised to find how difficult it was to keep pace with Mariel when she was going full steam. "For future reference, it does not require a lengthy sermon to persuade me to 'stick close' to a silver-tongued, generally appealing genius of a woman. Especially one who keeps ogling me."

"Thank you. I don't think I've ever been called 'generally appealing' before."

Even the most dedicated of rabbits would have thrown up its ears in defeat trying to navigate the array of offices, soundstages, trailers, and pre- and postproduction facilities that Mariel was able to guide them through without a false step. Nestled somewhere in this maze was a sort of auxiliary costume and makeup wing, attached in theory to two larger buildings, but accessible from neither. Mariel, naturally, knew where the actual entrance was.

She led Artie, in turn, through the interior maze of the building itself, bringing him at last into Henry's work area.

There sat Henry. And straddling Henry's lap was a redheaded woman who was very busy kissing Henry like hell.

"I thought you said he was a makeup specialist. This looks more like a make*out* specialist."

"Perhaps they had a spat. In that case, we could say they were making *up*, right?"

Mariel's voice, which had carried farther than Artie's, attracted Henry's attention. "Ah! Come in, come in." His companion halted her meal and winked at them.

"We don't want to interrupt you," said Mariel graciously.

"Midge has to get back to the front office anyway," said Henry. He squeezed Midge's chest as she leaned in for a goodbye kiss. "And what a nice front office it is," he said to her dotingly.

She hopped off of Henry and hurried past them, brushing them with perfume and enthusiasm.

It was only when Henry stood up that Artie realized what a giant of a man he was – a benign Goliath whose comforting smile cracked through his European-style beard, and whose huge but delicate hands Artie could easily imagine sculpting the details of a putty nose or an artificial birthmark. It occurred to him that the timid Lila might want Henry around as much for his reassuring presence as his talents.

"By the way, Midge and I are getting married soon. I hope I can count on both of you to be there," Henry said magnanimously, looking from Mariel to Artie.

"We'll be delighted!" said Mariel.

"I'm Artie," Artie added.

"Excellent." Henry backed up his approval of Artie's name, or existence, with a warm handshake. "Are you with Heffy, too?"

"Insofar as any of us are," said Mariel. She explained the situation.

"Sid Heffy is a genius," Henry boomed. "Who else could have realized that Heffy playing serious will be the funniest thing he's ever done?"

"I'm glad *you* think it's funny," said Mariel. "But – just for laughs – what would you do about it, if you were in our shoes?"

Henry stroked his chin. "Well, let's see …"

"Beg your pardon, Henry." A page had darted in so briskly that he'd nearly collided with Artie. "Miss Lowell needs you with the portable kit right away." The page darted out again without awaiting a reply.

"We'll talk to you later," said Mariel. "Give our regards to your rouge and lipstick."

# Chapter 5

As Mariel drove them off the lot, Artie turned awkwardly around to watch the studio wonderland receding.

"I always like talking to Lila and Henry when I'm faced with a problem or a decision," said Mariel. "But they're usually more helpful than this."

"To be fair, neither of them had much of a chance."

"True. Bad timing on our part.'"

"How about you?" Mariel asked, after a few more minutes of driving. "Do you have a routine when you're trying to decide how to get a grip on something?"

"Don't you mean some*one?*"

"Jeepers, Artie. Can't you keep your mind off sex for five minutes? You're as bad as I am."

"Compliment noted. But yes: back in New York, I did have my own special gimmick when mulling over a decision. It wasn't that different from yours, really."

"You had a friend you talked to?"

"Yes, you might say that. Only ..."

"Only what?"

He told her about Trixie.

"A mannequin, Artie? Oh, I do hope you're *not* kidding."

Mariel invited herself in to his apartment, and Artie made a pot of coffee.

"I'm very interested in your decision-making method," she said.

"You mean Trixie?"

"Yes. Now, I've never been to Macy's," Mariel confessed. "But let's see if I can help. I think you'll find the view is best if I use that little ladder." She pointed toward the corner in which she'd spied it.

Delighted by the game she was initiating, he brought the ladder to the center of the living room, and she mounted it with style.

"About like this?"

"Let's see." He crouched. "Oh yes, that's ... perfect." Mariel's legs held their stockings well, and the busywork of garters and satin tap pants looked fine indeed over the robust femininity of her thighs and crotch.

"Getting any ideas yet?"

"You bet I am."

"About our problem, I mean."

He craned his neck backward to make eye contact. "We have a problem?"

She smirked. "Maybe you can't see it from that angle. By the way, didn't you ever draw attention, crouching on the Macy's sidewalk?"

"People in New York mind their own business. I guess that's part of why I came out here – I was ready for a place where people are a little more in each other's hair."

"I can't wait for you to be in my hair."

He reached for her ankle. Far above him her bottom, so round in tight satin under the skirt, seemed to plead for an amorous slap.

He backed his head out to see her face again. Her eyes were closed, and she was smiling beatifically. "I like you, Artie."

He clasped her other ankle as well and kissed each calf, making her stockings damp. He could smell her arousal.

"Would you like to fuck me now?"

He emerged from the skirt and stood up. "You'll have to come down from there first."

He found he was able to lift her down with an arm around her waist and a bracing hand pressed against the satin smoothness of her tap-pants pussy. The tap pants felt warm.

"The bedroom is through there." He inclined his head.

"Walk slowly." She wiggled, grinding herself against his hand.

As she had requested, Artie took methodical, measured steps toward their destination. "I'd been wondering when you'd slow down enough for me to get my hands on you."

"I'd been wondering, too."

He deposited her, supine, on the bed, and sat next to her; but Mariel immediately rose up to claw at his trouser buttons. "Give me that cock, damn it. I've been itching to touch it for two days."

His erection intensified as her cool palm gripped and lifted it. He groaned with the satisfaction of being handled.

And when she began to bob here and there on the head and the shaft with restless kisses, the hot wetness of her mouth provided a fascinating contrast with her fingers.

"*Mmmm ... mmmm.*" Her moist commentary seemed to add extra lubrication to his rod. "I'm creaming my panties," she volunteered.

"Show me."

She rose from the bed to unhitch her skirt and kick off her shoes. This left her in stockings, garters, tap pants, blouse ... and cloche hat.

She peeled the tap pants down, handing them to Artie while he gawked at her nakedness. "See?"

He ran his fingers over the juicy gusset, and brought the satin to his nostrils. Oh yes, she had creamed her panties for him. She was the smartest, most animated person he'd ever known – and she'd slickened her goddamn tap pants in his honor. Put that way, the thought made him delirious.

Mariel removed the feather from her cloche – still leaving the hat on her head – and handed this to Artie as well. Then she lowered her bare ass to his lap.

He set the feather down for a moment, long enough to slap her gently on the ass and maneuver her backward. Lifting her lower half toward his face, he breathed on her thighs, relishing the nearness of her pussy. It waited there for him – so ready, so close, so beautifully pink and pouty.

He squirmed out from under her and retrieved the feather. Then, kneeling between her legs, he teased the hungry flesh midway between knees and cunt, eliciting quiet, erotic giggles as he titillated with the fluffy accessory.

"Hmmheeheehee ... I bet your mannequin couldn't oblige you by being ticklish like this."

"Hell, no," he acknowledged, while still softly tickling. "Trixie never even laughed at my jokes – though somehow I could tell by reading them to her whether they worked or not."

"More," Mariel instructed. He responded with some lengthier feather strokes, up toward her pussy on one side, then down to the knee joint on the other.

"Oh, that's nice," she giggled. "Oh my – oh fuck!" she shrieked with delight.

He chuckled along with her, the lust brimming in his throat.

"Hee-hee, oh, I have to tell you, Artie, there's – ee-hee-hee – there's one place along there where if you tickle me – just for three seconds, I swear – I'll totally lose it ... I'll orgasm, I'll pee myself from pleasure, I'll tell you I love you."

He hadn't thought he could get more aroused, but she was doing it to him.

"Your job – hee! – is to find that spot. But not today. I want you up my cunt, Artie. Now. Please."

Pausing only to fish a rubber out of his pocket and apply it, he discarded his jacket and grasped her by the knees, his glans testing her opening. She forked her fingers around his dick to guide him as she opened wider, pressing her other hand against his trouser seat to urge him deeper.

Pleasure melted through him as he filled her; and as he descended onto her chest, she whined her own joy in his face like a motor in heat.

With one hand on his waist now and the other still glued to his ass, Mariel held Artie with impressive power, channeling her phenomenal supply of energy into clenching and working him, into squeezing his cock with her cunt muscles and churning her body around his axis, describing tiny circles beneath his weight.

The rhythm of Artie's thrusts was a response to the momentum of the fucking, rather than its driving force. Mariel was the engine, applying every ounce of her lust to the enterprise in the same way she applied her resources to everything she undertook. Artie's arousal, his joy and his ecstasy, were hitched to Mariel's sexual animus as snugly as his cock was locked in her sex, and with almost no effort on his part, he felt himself fucking for all he was worth. If a fuck had ever felt this good before, this all-consuming, it was a memory that the present experience had already wiped out.

She didn't need much from him, and yet she needed everything from him. *His* cock in her pussy. *His* thumb on her clit. *His* hand squeezing her ass cheek, and *his* fingers venturing into the crack. Articulating these thoughts in his head sent Artie over the edge; and Mariel, evidently sensing that he was poised for release, let herself go – humping her hips upward to trap his thumb where it sparked her button, then coming like an animal beneath him.

"Why don't you come with me to Heffy headquarters, to return the auto? Then we can get a streetcar back to town and grab some lunch."

"Good idea. I didn't even think I was hungry ... but your appetite gives me an appetite."

As they traveled to Heffy's, they continued examining the prospects of the immediate future.

"You know," said Mariel as they pulled into the driveway, "there's one person who might be even more concerned about all this than we are."

"Some devoted listener?"

"You could call her that, yes."

As if on cue, Elyse ran out of the house to greet them.

"It's impossible! What are we to do, Mariel?"

She insinuated her elegant form into the driver's seat, causing Mariel, in turn, to squeeze her petite frame into the hollow bounded by Artie's bony hip and his knobby shoulder. Her bottom encroached pleasantly on his lap, and she rested both her hands on his forearm.

"Not much fun there without us?" said Mariel sympathetically.

Elyse blinked back tears as she backed the car out. "Yesterday, my life was perfect: a house full of laughter-conjuring, clitoris-pleasing heroes. Apart from the nuisance of having to keep my clothes on whenever Daddy was around, the place was paradise on earth."

She paused for breath.

"Now, today, you're all gone, and what do I get? Daddy in his most pretentious mood, and that dreadful man from the playhouse. *Lionel Stimpson*," she said with distaste.

"Simpson?" asked Artie.

"No, *Stimpson*," Elyse insisted, her tone implying that the *t* made it that much worse.

"Is he so awful?" asked Mariel.

Elyse snorted. Artie noted how rare a talent it was for someone to be able to do this in a way that sounded pretty; but the sex goddess had pulled it off. "He's got Daddy doing a three-act play – in god knows how many weekly installments – and there's not a single joke in the whole horrible thing. Not even a witticism or a bon mot."

"All those *mots*, and not a single one that's even a little bit *bon*?" said Mariel.

"I tell you, there isn't. And as for Lionel Stimpson personally – what a colossal pill. Which is no surprise, of course. He corrects everything anyone else says – whether it's fact, opinion, or *gesundheit*. I swear, if this arrangement doesn't change, I'm likely to go into pictures after all, just to get out of the house."

Mariel looked at Artie, her eyes shimmering with brilliance, before turning back to Elyse. "Or ... ," she began portentously, "how about going into radio?"

"Radio? But no one could *see* me on the radio."

"That's true, alas. But consider this: Your father is a rather conceited man, wouldn't you agree?"

"*Rather* conceited? No. If you'd like to amend that to *extremely* conceited, then we might have an agreement."

"I really do have to meet Mr. Heffy one of these days," Artie interjected. "If only as part of a well-rounded education."

"So then," Mariel continued, "how do you think Sid would react if someone else – someone from his own family – were suddenly competing with him for attention? On-the-air attention, that is."

"*On-the-air-attention*," Artie echoed reflectively, instinctively endorsing Mariel's train of thought even as he tried to follow it.

"What are you two talking about?" said Elyse.

"Yeah," said Artie. "What are we talking about?"

"I'm talking about *The Elyse Heffernan Show*."

"What! You mean do my own show? To compete with Daddy?"

"Exactly."

"But ... well, I'd need writers, wouldn't I?"

"I think I know where we can get ahold of your favorite ones."

Elyse's face lit up. "Wouldn't I need a sponsor?"

"Artie and I have already laid the groundwork for that."

"We have?"

"Sure. Down at the lot this morning. We just didn't realize it at the time."

# Chapter 6

"Speaking of sponsors," said Artie into his sandwich, "isn't *Heffy's* sponsor likely to veto this Lionel Stimpson monstrosity?"

They had piled into a corner bench at the luncheonette, with Mariel flanked by the others.

"As it happens," she explained, "the woman who owns Dressinger Clothing is one of the few tycoons in America who cares more about culture than about money." She turned to Elyse. "And the tragedy is, she's just the type of sucker who will mistake the efforts of your Mr. Stimpson for culture."

"Please, darling," complained Elyse, "he's not *my* Mr. Stimpson."

"Well, whoever he belongs to ... Lentilla Dressinger – yes, Artie, *Dressinger* is really the woman's name – is sure to think his *work* belongs to the ages. The worse we think it is, no doubt the more profound she will deem it to be. Moreover, I have a suspicion it may have been Dressinger herself who first suggested to Heffy that he might try his chubby hand at capital-D drama, on company time."

"But you think we're already on our way to finding a sponsor of our own," said Artie.

"Yes." Mariel looked at her wristwatch. "We'll follow up on that this evening."

Elyse, having finished her meal, wiped her sensuous mouth with what, in her hands, gave the impression of being a sensuous napkin.

"You're actually going to write comedy for *me*?" She indulged in a visible shudder of contentment.

"Judging from Miss Heffernan's ecstasy – as measured by the hip that's vibrating vigorously against my own – I think we have a winner of a scheme here. What do you think, Artie?"

"I think that next time we all go to lunch, I want to sit in the middle."

"Fair enough," said Mariel. "But allow me to transmit the vital information, for the nonce. The ecstatic, vibrating hip felt like this." She jiggled on the bench, duly delivering the tremors to Artie. She punctuated the procedure by gripping his thigh.

Elyse tittered – which Artie noticed made her nose wiggle – and deliberately initiated another round of shimmies. Artie, never one to weasel out of pulling his weight, jerked his hip bone against Mariel.

"Ooh! The middle *is* fun," she attested.

Artie noticed their waiter engaging his attention via arched eyebrow.

"You folks need anything?" the waiter inquired, coming nearer. He was attentive but unfazed – a veteran Hollywood waiter, in all likelihood.

"Just a network and a time slot," said Mariel.

The waiter shrugged. "Who knows, it could happen ... I've seen worse acts come through here. Of course, for radio, you'll need an announcer to explain what's going on with all that wriggling and jiggling."

"Thanks for the tip," said Mariel. "Hollywood is the only place where the waiters tip the customers," she informed Artie.

After Elyse had settled up, Mariel got back to business. "Elyse, you wouldn't be shy about phoning Mickey, would you? To officially state that you want to hire Sid's former writing team?"

"Shy ... about Mickey? Mickey *Licky?*" Elyse rolled her head back in laughter, looking slightly surprised when she bumped it on the wall. "In fact," she continued, "never mind phoning. Do you realize it's been almost twenty-four hours since anyone touched my pussy – besides me, I mean? I think I'll visit Mickey in person."

"An excellent idea," said Mariel. "Artie and I can walk from here."

"We can? Where are we going?" The luncheonette wasn't close to Mariel's place or his own.

"Somewhere within walking distance."

A nearby park fulfilled that criterion.

"Writing for Elyse should be interesting," Artie remarked as they strolled.

"Yes – she's a totally different type from her father. Thank goodness."

"What's the angle, as you see it?" Artie knew very well that, for the most part, you couldn't write the same material for any two performers: you had to match the jokes to the personality. And in a case like this – where the star had no established shtick, no vaudeville act or movie career defining her – you had to figure out what the personality *was*, comedically speaking. In fact, you had to take an active role in shaping it, sculpting the character with your words as you went along.

"Elyse is pure sex."

"I've noticed."

"We're going to use that. We'd best not do it overtly, on the radio. But we'll do it every which way *except* overtly."

Artie nodded emphatically. "Brilliant – I see exactly what you mean. And where does the comedy come in?"

"It's already there. Elyse is so sex-obsessed it's funny. And the funniness in itself is sexy. In my view, the two elements reinforce each other, especially when you consider how likeable she is. Elyse Heffernan, the friendly neighborhood sex goddess. She loves to laugh, and we'll have her laugh at herself. People will laugh with her, drooling to fuck her all the while – or fuck the appealing male characters we'll surround her with."

"Elyse is going to enjoy that – all of America wanting to fuck her."

"You bet she is. And here's the other thing: Elyse is smart. Like Mae West, but ethereal rather than earthy. Like Lila Lowell, but impassioned rather than jaded. We'll give her wisecracks and witty insights – never neglecting the double entendres and innuendo, of course – and turn the 'dumb bimbo' thing on its head. Oh, this is going to be sensational, Artie! Elyse will be the hottest thing on the pleasure dial. I'm so excited, I could pee."

"I mark that's the third time in our young friendship you've made an out-of-context allusion to peeing. This is not a complaint, mind you – merely an observation."

"See, that's another advantage I have over Trixie – man-nequins don't pee."

"But getting back to *The Elyse Heffernan Show*: I have to hand it to you. I was considered a pretty sharp idea guy in New York. But you don't just think in ideas, you think in Concepts with a capital C. My hat goes off to you."

"And your pants, too, I've been pleased to note. But Thank You, Artie – with a capital T. And you know what? I think I really *do* have to pee. *In* context."

He thought she would reverse direction so they could stroll back toward the public conveniences. Instead, she stepped onto the grass, retrieving a cream-colored handker-chief from her skirt pocket. As she lowered herself into a squat, she sent a hankie flourish his way, as though she were waving *bonjour* (and definitely not *au revoir*) from the deck of an ocean liner.

"Right here? But someone will see you."

"I sure hope so," said Mariel.

He instinctively averted his eyes.

"You're kidding, Artie," she said with disappointment, as faint sounds documented the displacement of skirt and lingerie. "Oh, well, lead a horse to water ..."

As she enunciated the last word, he heard the beginnings of her stream trickling down to the ground. And having absorbed the indisputable evidence that she *wanted* him to look on while she watered the grass, he decided to unavert his eyes.

"Oh," chirped Mariel, "are you back? The show's just started, good seats down front." She broke into laughter as a shudder of pleasure cut into her narrative. "Ahahahaha. Oh, bliss! Honestly, sometimes I think sprinkling is better than sex."

*"Sprinkling," nothing*, thought Artie – Mariel was now pouring like a spout. No one had ever shown him before how thickly, how forcefully a woman could pee. The torrent of release was a revelation overwhelming in its majestic – and, he found, intensely erotic – beauty. The acute, intimate ecstasy she was evidently taking from the process brought him a shudder of his own, a tickle of arousal that seemed to travel from his balls up the spine to his shoulder blades. His eyes were now locked on her river, his mind contemplating the pleasure Mariel was feeling between her legs.

When she sighed and reached up and inward to wipe herself with the handkerchief, he felt as if she were pulling her fist up the length of his dick.

There was nobody else in sight. "Give me that," he requested quickly, before he'd even thought about what he was saying.

Mariel stood, grinning with enthusiasm, and handed him the streaked hankie.

"Oh, god," he said appreciatively, bringing it to his face to savor the rich aromas of cunt and fresh, feminine pee.

In another instant his cock was out of his pants, wrapped in the woman-wetted cloth. He jerked himself off in a half-dozen strokes while she watched him, answering his frenzied grunts with delighted "oohs."

"We liked that, didn't we?" she said when he'd finished.

As they'd arranged, Mariel came to Artie's place at seven that night so they could drop in on Lila at home. He was struggling with a book on golf when she arrived.

"You're interested in golf?"

"About as interested as I am in stepping in a mud puddle. In other words, it's an experience I'm not eager to seek out, but one I'm sure I'll encounter sooner or later. That's why I picked this book up at Penn Station; I figured once I got out here, it wouldn't be long before someone insisted I go golfing. And I don't want to make a fool of myself."

"No."

"I mean, I'm sure I *will* make a fool of myself . . . but why do it right out of the gate? Though I might, at that – I was taking some practice swings with a broom in the courtyard earlier, and I'm pretty sure that if there'd been a ball involved, it would've been flying in the wrong direction."

"Hmm ... maybe your form is imperfect," she said tactfully.

He laughed. "Yes, maybe my form is imperfect." He threw the book on the sofa. "Come on, let's go."

They walked out to the courtyard and, from there, to the corner to hail a cab.

"Did you phone Lila?" Artie asked, once they were underway.

"Lila doesn't use a phone."

"She doesn't have one?"

"She doesn't have one *and* she doesn't use one. It intimidates her."

"Ah, I see," said Artie. "Are you sure we'll be welcome as uninvited guests?"

"I told you – Lila is always expecting me, in a general way. She lives in a perpetual state of expecting me."

"That must be exhausting."

"One develops a strength for it, like with swimming."

"Speaking of swimming, I wonder how Elyse made out with Mickey."

"I'm sure we needn't wonder. Unless you meant *how* in the sense of 'which position?'"

"I confess I didn't. But shall we discuss that awhile, as long as we're stuck in this cab?"

"Ooh, I love a good parlor game. Your thoughts?"

He settled more comfortably into the taxi's upholstery, putting his arm around Mariel. "Well, as a starting point, she did give us a hint with that 'Mickey Licky' gag. And I noticed, the one day we all worked together, what finesse Mickey has as a writer. He's extremely precise. So I can see him really finessing Elyse, working meticulously on her with his tongue, until she screams very beautifully."

Mariel shifted in place, bumping his chest with her shoulder. "Very nice, Artie. I can see that too. I can even feel it." She closed her eyes for a moment.

"Your turn," said Artie.

"I'm thinking about how tall and lithe Elyse is, while Mickey is built small and sturdy. If she were to ride him, the picture we'd see would be something like 75 percent Elyse and 25 percent Mickey. But he's strong – strong and solid." Mariel warmed to her theme, drawing on her imagination – or, perhaps, her experience – to describe the head writer more vividly. "He's a tight little dynamo of muscle and stability. His cock is thick and steely in her snatch, anchoring the extensive, fluid anatomy of our goddess as she skewers herself on him, with her torso undulating and her arms flailing and her hair wild around her even wilder face."

"Fuck," Artie grunted. Mariel put her hand in his crotch, testing the effects of her narrative.

"Go ahead," she prompted.

"Let's have Elyse lie down now – she must be tired."

"Elyse? Ha!"

"Let's have her lie down regardless. Facedown on the bed. Damn, what a statuesque bottom that woman has."

"Check."

"Mickey could caress that bottom all night."

"Remember, she went to see him during the day."

"All right, then, all day. I can visualize her creamy flesh as he sculpts it. I can feel how warm it is." He gestured, his hands poised as if to squeeze two magnificent cheeks. "The hue drifts a bit toward pink as he stimulates every inch of her skin there. And when he tickles the crack she dances for him, grinding her mound into the mattress while her derriere does the rumba in his face."

"My" – Mariel took a deep breath – "turn." She inhaled again. "Oh, Artie, I'm juicing the hell out of my underwear."

She was still clutching him through his pants, his cock a hard, horizontal lever in her grasp.

He let his hand creep up her leg until it found the sensitive softness of her lingerie. "Maybe we'd better ..." he began.

The cab came to a halt. They had arrived.

"We'll finish this ... discussion ... later," she said weakly. "Okay?"

He nodded.

Artie stood cooling off in the evening air, willing his erection to go dormant, while he listened to Mariel's conversation with the cabbie.

"What do we owe you?"

"That depends on the upkeep, miss. Any wet spots back there after your little roundtable discussion?"

"Keep the change," said Mariel.

# Chapter 7

Where Sid Heffy's mansion was along the lines of how a tourist would envision a Hollywood star's home – the butler, the swimming pool, the array of elegantly furnished rooms – Lila Lowell's house would have disappointed the typical starstruck mansion-gawker.

To begin with, it was modest in size. Granted, one could argue that the garden – or rather jungle – whose palms dwarfed the house from behind, and whose vegetation also enclosed the building on both sides, counterbalanced this to some extent. But not counting the dizzying palms, the residence comprised only a single story. And there was no garage.

Were a starstruck mansion-gawker to venture through the front door, said individual would be further disappointed by the fact that nearly every available inch of the star's home was filled with overstuffed bookshelves, leaving very little room for the orgies one liked to imagine taking place on the home turf of any self-respecting screen idol. A fan whose fantasies revolved around orgies of *reading*, on the other hand, would undoubtedly orgasm on the spot.

Artie was still endeavoring *not* to orgasm on the spot as Lila escorted them into her claustrophobic living room, and he gathered Mariel was in a similar condition. He was finding the unreleased sexual tension pleasant in its own right – a tingle of extended excitement and delayed gratification. Since arriving in Hollywood only three days earlier, it seemed he'd spent more time being titillated, aroused, and gratified – and returning these favors for Mariel and Elyse – than he'd spent engaged in similar activities in the entire past year in New York. Perhaps this was the change he'd been unconsciously seeking when he said farewell to Trixie, Macy's, and Manhattan.

Lila, who had not yet spoken in the course of greeting them and ushering them in, seated herself at a small table that boasted a checkerboard.

"Play with me while we talk," she requested quietly of Mariel.

Mariel took her place at the table, and Artie availed himself of a third chair that hovered haphazardly to one side. His erection, though not the massive encumbrance it had been a few minutes earlier, was still hanging in there, and the slope of the wooden chair seat allowed Artie to appease his sensitized hardness through a bit of direct contact, by dint of straddling the chair and leaning forward.

Mariel, he noticed, had her thighs squeezed tightly together, perhaps to treat her clit to a bit of *indirect* pressure through layers of cloth and feminine flesh. As the subdued click-clack of a checker game commenced, she broached the evening's business.

"Lila, we now have a strategy for solving the Sid Heffy radio-drama problem."

Lila nodded, smiling.

"And your assistance could be instrumental."

"Of course," said Lila, almost inaudibly, but without hesitation. She looked directly at Artie for the first time since their arrival. "I'd do just about anything for Mariel."

Artie nodded his approval and concurrence.

"Thank you, Lila," said Mariel. "All you'd have to do is sponsor a radio show for a few weeks."

"Sponsor?" Her surprise was reflected in the midair dangling of a checker en route to being retired from the board. "But I don't own a business," she murmured.

"You don't need a business. All you need is money – which, last I knew, you had plenty of."

"I still don't get it," Artie confessed. "You mean *The Elyse Heffernan Show* would say 'sponsored by Lila Lowell'?"

"Elyse Heffernan?" Lila's face lit up, and her voice almost broke into the sultry timbre of the on-screen Lila. "That Venus with angel wings?"

Down in Culver City, Artie recalled, Mariel had hinted at Lila's interests: "for those of us with a taste for male individuals" was how she'd qualified her praise of his animal magnetism. Lila's evident enthusiasm for sponsoring Elyse, over and above her simple willingness to help her friends foil Heffy, resonated with the supposition that no matter how many interchangeable mustached men Lila might involve herself with at the cinema, it was women who lit her quietly tended fire in private life.

Additional support for this theory entered the room the next moment.

"Hello, Nanette," said Mariel.

"Hello, Marry. And this must be Artie. Hello, Artie."

Nanette had large, liquid eyes, dirty-blond hair in ringlets, and plump lips. In contrast to the modesty of Lila's at-home loungewear – the actress sat at the checkerboard in a handsome but unrevealing housecoat – Nanette had made her entrance in the merest of undies. Artie judged her to be a bit older than Lila – about forty – with the appearance some people had of becoming increasingly sexy as they progressed through life. Her gait, as she walked to Lila's side, suggested she could already feel her lover's hands roving her body.

"I'll come to bed soon," Lila promised. She waddled her chair backward – a maneuver that, Artie observed, even an elegant movie star could not make gracefully – to allow Nanette enough room to kneel and to rest her head in Lila's lap. It meant abandoning the checker game, but from where Artie sat it looked like a fine trade.

"We'll try to be quick," said Mariel. "As the sponsor, you'll be anonymous, Lila. Or rather, your identity will be concealed behind a business name. A name that we make up for that purpose."

"Won't people know that's fishy?" said Artie. "Everyone recognizes the companies that sponsor radio programs."

"Yes, I've thought of that. That's why we're going to invent a company that doesn't sell things directly to the public. Think about it: As you've pointed out, everyone knows who makes iceboxes and automobiles and soap. But the people who make all those things have suppliers for *their* materials – and unless you were in the business, you'd have no idea who *those* companies were."

"Smart," whispered Lila. Nanette lifted her head temporarily to nod in agreement.

"But why would those kinds of companies advertise on the radio?" Artie asked.

Mariel shrugged. "Why do big businesses do half the crazy things they do? No one will question it. All we need to do is come up with an idea for a company that makes something that other companies use."

"I've got it!" said Artie. "Mannequins."

Mariel laughed. "Oh, you and your Trixie."

"Who's Trixie?" asked Nanette.

"Trixie is Artie's best mannequin back home."

"I mean it, Mariel. Department stores all over the country are obviously buying mannequins from somebody. But do any of us know who's making them?"

Lila and Nanette exchanged glances. "*We* don't," volunteered Nanette.

"If Trixie had a brand name imprinted on her behind, I assure you I would be aware of it," Artie added conclusively.

Mariel looked thoughtful. "Mannequins, eh? 'The Metropolitan Mannequin Company presents *The Elyse Heffernan Show*.'" She giggled at their creation, but she was nodding with enthusiasm. "Yes, Artie. Yes!"

Artie was rather pleased with himself.

"Got a pencil?" Mariel continued. "Write this down. *Metropolitan Mannequins: Magnificent mannequins for the modern world.* That'll be our tagline."

"Remember, she used to be a publicist," Lila commented to Nanette.

"Congratulations, Lila," said Mariel, beaming. "You're in business."

# Chapter 8

There was a festive atmosphere around the Heffernan pool the next morning, when Sid's discarded writing team assembled to craft his daughter's inaugural script. Lubb's raised eyebrows had been swiftly returned to rest position by the star-to-be, whose affability was so potent that even the surly butler sought to please her.

The boys had donned their swimsuits at the suggestion of their new employer, who had greeted them in a jade-green bathing costume of advanced – and minimalist – design, a garment that relied on flirtatious fringes to make its limited coverage ever so slightly less limited.

"I didn't know it was formal," Mariel teased, indicating Artie's black trunks. The other men's swimsuits were a lush forest of plaids. "I guess you can take the boy out of New York ..."

"You're a fine one to talk," he quipped back. "Aren't you going to get undressed like the rest of us?" Mariel looked dashing but anomalous in her usual skirt, blazer, and cloche.

"No, I get chilly too easily. Any seminakedness on my part will have to be confined to the indoors."

"Fair enough," said Artie.

With this procedural point settled, Mariel turned to Mickey. "Mind if I take the typewriter today? I'd sort of like to have my hands on this."

"But then who's going to pace and wave that feather?" asked Artie.

"You may have the honor," said Mariel, removing the object from her hat and presenting it to her deputy with great ceremony. The others applauded, and Mariel took a bow.

His knowledge of where the feather had recently been gave Artie a little thrill as he took charge of it.

After Mariel had offered her general vision for the show's premise and personality, the writers quickly found their collective rhythm – and the star found hers, making a point of perching on the lap of whichever writer held the floor, wiggling with glee as she listened to each humorous idea. Only Benny – whom Elyse invited to bring a gentleman of his choice next time for lap-perching – and Mariel – who was occupied with the typewriter – were exempted from this routine. Artie, who was fulfilling his sacred obligations by pacing with feather whenever he orated, received an adapted version of the treatment, whereby Elyse kept a step ahead of him, stopping shortly after every joke so that his swimsuit would bump her bottom as she laughed.

"Okay, then how about this ... ?"

Elyse quickly hopped off of Mickey's lap and situated herself in Gabe's.

"Her lawyer says, 'If you wish to sell that racehorse, we simply cannot delay this paperwork any longer. I must have it out by Wednesday.' And she says, 'I promise, Skinny.'"

"Skinny?" Mariel interrupted. "Since when is the lawyer called 'Skinny'?"

"I think it sounds good," said Gabe. "Short *i* sounds are funny. 'I promise, Skinny,' she says. 'Come Monday morning, my mind will be on that bill of sale and in that office.'"

"Yeah," said Benny. "And the lawyer says, 'Very good, Miss Scarsdale. I'll look forward to seeing your mind here at nine o'clock Monday. Oh, and I do hope your *body* will be here as well.'" Benny delivered the line with the requisite hint of lasciviousness.

Everyone laughed, and Elyse bounced merrily on Gabe's swimsuit, playing with the fur on his chest.

"Wait!" said Mariel. "We can top that. Maestro, the quill."

Artie began keeping time for her, with as much gravitas as could be managed by a man wearing a bathing suit and using a feather as a baton.

"Elyse says ... 'No, my body is busy on Mondays.' 'Busy?' he says. 'Yes,' she says. 'It has a part-time job as a busybody.'"

Again the assembled broke up.

"Yeah!" said Artie. "Only ... what do you say we change it to Thursday? Thursdays are funnier than Mondays."

"I don't know," Mariel mused. "If we make the *day* too funny, it could distract from the punch line."

"And anyway, I think Wednesdays are funniest," said Mickey.

"I've always favored Tuesday," said Howard.

The lively debate that ensued was interrupted by the arrival of Mr. Sid Heffy, star of film and radio comedy, serious-actor-in-training, and owner of the premises.

Elyse rose to greet him. "Hello, Daddy."

The privilege of finally laying eyes on Sid Heffy – a dubious one, under present circumstances – emphasized to Artie the difference between this personage and the sketchy imitation known as Lubb. Heffy's presence was cartoonishly vivid: every muscle in his slightly rotund body and egg-shaped head was expressive. His face, at the moment, was a cartoon mask of indignation, coated with a thin veneer of disdain and a dusting of wounded vanity. In short, it was everything they'd counted on.

"What's the idea of bringing this crowd back here to haunt my house?" he began.

It was obvious to Artie right away that Sid's ex-writers found it hard to take him seriously, even when he was playing straight. Snickers were suppressed, knowing glances were exchanged, and eyeballs danced with amusement.

"Didn't Lubb tell you?" Elyse carried the weight of earnestness for the entire crew. "We're creating a new program – for me!"

"I thought that was Lubb's thin idea of a joke."

"But Daddy, you've been encouraging me for years to do something with my talents."

Artie watched her with admiration. She was playing ingenuous quite skillfully.

"I told you to get into pictures!" Heffy huffed. "Not this nonsense."

Mariel spoke up. "Look, Sid, someone has to provide the nonsense, now that you've been called to a higher art."

"I'm not going to stand here arguing with my employees."

"But Daddy ... they're *my* employees now."

"The whole thing's stupidiculous," said Heffy, lapsing into his world-famous performing vocabulary. "How these dunderheads can work with you distracting them all the time has always been a mystery to me, anyway."

"They work *better* when she 'distracts' them," Mariel interjected.

"Well, whether they work better or worse doesn't make one lima bean of difference," said Heffy, "'cause you'll never find a sponsor. Elyse is an unknown ..."

"That's a horrid thing to call your own daughter," said Elyse with chilly dignity.

"... and if any of you ... *cummerbunds*" – this was Heffy's most world-famous stock insult – "think for one second I'm going to use my influence in support of this harebrained idea, you – "

Mariel cut in again. "She *has* a sponsor, Sid."

This stopped him in his pudgy tracks. "What! Who?"

"Metropolitan Mannequins," Mariel said evenly, as though she were saying "General Electric" or "Campbell's Soup."

"Yeah? You just wait until I get in touch with that outfit."

"You may find that difficult," said Mariel. "I understand their management hierarchy is a well-kept secret. The mannequin biz is like that," she added knowingly.

"Oh, a *secret*, huh? Not to Sid Heffy it won't be."

No one had warned Artie that Sid spoke of himself in the third person. But he realized he ought to have anticipated it. And he wondered at what stage in a pompous star's career this habit was typically adopted. Perhaps there was a ceremony associated with it – a rite of passage.

"I have connections at every network. *Big* connections. They'll tell me who's signing the sponsor's checks."

With Sid's back toward them while he turned his glowering stare on Mickey, Artie shot Mariel a worried glance. He was new to this world, but he didn't think having Sid on her ass was part of the bargain Lila had agreed to. For an instant, Mariel's eyes reflected his own panic. Then they took on the look of inspired mischief he was already well familiar with.

"All right, Sid. There's no need to get nasty. I didn't want to involve Mr. ... uh ... Trix – Mr. *Trixton* ... but it so happens our sponsor is right here: the president of the Metropolitan Mannequin Company."

She was indicating Artie. *Of course!* he thought. *Sid has never seen me before.* His appreciation for Mariel – a woman whose wits, it was more and more apparent, were as sharp as her wit – further deepened. He was so impressed that it took him a full two seconds to feel the cold sweat of being thrust into an awkward, ludicrous charade without the slightest warning.

"*This* is a sponsor? In a bathing suit?"

"A *formal* bathing suit," Mariel snapped. "Mr. Trixton is so enthusiastic about Elyse's program that he insisted on sitting in on our first writing session. Isn't that correct, Mr. Trixton?"

"Yes," said Artie. "Absolutely."

Sid glared at him for an uncomfortably extended moment. "All right. It's obvious I'm not going to get anywhere trying to persuade you to drop this project, mister, since clearly you're thick as thieves with this gang. All right, then. Go ahead. Put my daughter on the air with your lousy jokes. Embarrass my whole family, from California to the cousins in the old country."

Artie judged this particular addendum to be extraneous, as he was willing to bet Sid didn't normally give much thought to the cousins in the old country – such as when distributing the profits of his art, for instance.

"Lose yourself a bundle in mannequins, Mr. Sponsor – then you'll pull out, you'll see. Now, if you'll excuse me ... since this area of *my* house is *occupied*, I'd better find somewhere to rehearse *The Sidney Heffy Dramatic Culture Hour*. Because *that* show is in for the long haul."

He made his exit.

"He really oughtn't have stressed both *my* and *occupied*," Mariel critiqued. "It disrupts the rhythm of the whole line."

Mickey's attention was riveted on a different detail from the speech. "Did he say culture *hour*? That piece of shit's going to be on for an *hour* every week?"

"That *will* be a long haul," said Mariel. "For the listeners." She turned to Artie with a sly smile. "Don't you agree, Mr. Trixton?"

After the writing session broke up, Mariel continued typing. "We don't want any loose ends," she explained. "Do you mind waiting for me?"

"Not at all," said Artie. "I have to change back into my street clothes anyway."

"Would you mind waiting to do *that*, too? I can just see your long, lean torso out of the corner of my eye ... and it's motivating me to work faster."

When she'd finally returned the portable typewriter to its case, Mariel's eyes scoured the pool area. "Where's my feather?" she asked.

"Oh!" said Artie. "Damn, I don't know. I must have set it down somewhere when Heffy burst in."

"I don't see it."

"No, neither do I. I'm sorry."

"Don't worry. I have a jewelry box full of them. Why don't you go change, and we can get out of here."

Once in the house, Artie took a wrong turn on his way to the bathroom where he'd left his clothes, accidentally heading toward the library instead. He was about to reverse course when he heard a compelling sound from beyond the closed library door: the sound of laughter – lazy, but undeniably sexual, female laughter.

*Heeheeheehee ... hmm-hmm ... oh!-a-heeheeheehee ...*

He immediately visualized Mariel's bountiful quill. This would account for its absence – someone was enjoying the gentle bliss of being tickled with it. Precisely where, he could only imagine.

Unless, of course, it was merely Elyse recalling her favorite bits from today's script session.

*HeeHEEh'heeeeee. Oh, yes, Howie, my pussy lips – the feather, the – ooh, yes yes, tickle my pussy, ti-iiiiiiiheeheeheehee ...*

Feather: check. Elyse: check. That was definitely her voice – and Artie thought she was doing a commendable job of improvising, playing a scene that had certainly not been in today's script.

He automatically slipped a hand into a conveniently located swimsuit pocket.

"What program are we listening to?"

Mariel had tiptoed up behind him, and suddenly her arm was around his waist and her voice in his ear.

He cocked his head. She sidled around him so as to hear better, and he watched the smile broaden on her face as she became oriented to the content of the entertainment.

"Do you think it's wrong of us to listen?" he whispered.

"Not where Elyse is concerned – and, by extension, anyone she consorts with. She'd love to know we were listening. In fact, I'll make a note to tell her, later on."

Her gaze drifted down to Artie's swim trunks. "You got a head start on me, didn't you?" She yanked Artie's hand from the pocket, replacing it with her own – at the same time maneuvering her body behind him, to urge herself against the muscles of his buttocks. His bare feet shifted with lewd, silent ecstasy on the carpet runner.

*I bet those lovely titties would like a little feathering too, mmm?*

Howard's voice, a flat monotone in the writing room, had a more liquid, insinuating quality under recreational circumstances.

*Oooh-hee, ooh-HEEEE, yes-y-eeeeee ... You're gonna make me c-c –*

"Oh, fuck, Artie, I can't wait." Mariel spun him around and wedged him up against the wall opposite the library. She'd found the rubber in his other bathing-suit pocket; Artie had decided from the first day in this environment that it would be convenient to keep them in each and every garment.

She sprang his cock out of the trunks with one hand while shoving her panties down with the other, nimbly stepping out of them while raising her skirt. Artie slapped her ass and pulled her tight against his chest, hoping to communicate with her nipples through blazer, blouse, and bra.

With the rubber in place, she was now struggling to mount him – Artie saw that she had not staged the scene felicitously, given their height difference. He loved her assertiveness, but she'd have to practically climb him like a tree to get her cunt around his cock. "Let's switch places," he advised.

"Mmmgh," she agreed.

This was more like it. Mariel braced herself against the wall, while Artie bent at the knees and lifted her by her hot little ass-cheeks.

Though they'd been pacing this as a frenzied sprint, they slowed down as her lubricated flesh inched its way onto him, both parties devotedly silent while each discrete instant of sensation filtered from their junction through their pleasure-response systems.

"You feel as good as *she* sounds," Artie whispered when the connection was complete, knowing Mariel would approve of the remark. Sure enough, the comparison seemed to further energize her blazing libido. Taking advantage of the wall at her back and the hands on her ass, she wrapped her legs around Artie's thighs, steadied herself on his shoulders, and used every ounce of her strength to squeeze her horny cunt up and down his shaft – now bouncing, now lingering, fucking her bottom off while Elyse's shrieks and giggles reverberated in the background.

A sustained alto wail from Mariel's lips told Artie she was getting very close. Sure enough, her left hand disappeared from his shoulder and joined the party down south, claiming its mistress's clit. With her weight fully supported by his arms and his dick ready to explode any second, Artie had an inspiration.

Relying on her rhythm for momentum, he took the few backward steps necessary to cross the hallway, then pivoted in midfuck. "Turn the doorknob," he muttered urgently. Mariel complied instantly, streaking the knob with girl juice from her clitty finger.

Everything happened at once. The door swung open and Elyse, who was radiantly naked, screamed in climax, her eyes widening with extra delight as she registered her audience. Writhing on the library sofa, she extracted every atom of pleasure from the quill Howard held to her crotch, while Mariel pogo-sticked on Artie's cock, her endless orgasmic moan almost as loud as the blonde goddess's scream. Artie pumped and pumped inside the hug of Mariel's thighs, his buttocks muscles working in double time and his hands holding her bottom cheeks with such passion that he felt her flesh molding itself around his fingers.

*The Elyse Heffernan Show* was definitely off to a good start, Artie noted, as he crumpled to the floor with Mariel in his lap. She was still slowly undulating.

# Chapter 9

This time, they ended their day in Mariel's apartment – the most notable feature of which was that most every surface from bedroom to kitchen was strewn with radio scripts, representing every comedy program Artie had ever heard or heard *of*.

Had this been the home of a lesser writer, Artie might have suspected the resident of joke stealing; but in this case the idea was so absurd as to make him smile as he instantly dismissed it. No, Mariel was a scholar, not a thief. And a damn resourceful one – these scripts couldn't be easy to come by.

"What next?" Artie asked, over a Scotch.

"Well, we need to line up a network, of course. That won't be any trouble with our sponsor on board, but we need to consider who can get us on the air when, and in what time slot. Directly opposite Heffy on a competing network would be perfect."

"Right."

"We should also kill off Mr. Trixton as soon as possible, now that he's served his purpose."

"I wish you'd rephrase that. Remember, Trixton is *me*."

"Yes, that's the problem."

"I thought I handled myself rather well, given the short notice."

She kissed him on the nose. "You were marvelous, and I'm sure *Variety* will rave about you in the morning.

But I need you on that writing team – not to mention various other places in my life and on my person – and we don't want Sid to find out he's been hoodwinked."

"Ah. Yes, I see what you mean. But can't we just work someplace other than the Heffernan estate?"

"Yes, we can and we will. But that's not enough. Sid is sure to find out where Elyse is operating from, and drop by unexpectedly to monitor her progress."

"And I'll be right there. Hmm ... can we pretend that Mr. Trixton is such an enthusiast, he attends *every* writing session?"

"Too risky – especially if he catches you in flagrante giving us a good line. Sid's not the quickest study, but like most old vaudevillians he makes up for any intellectual weaknesses with a gloriously suspicious imagination. I think he'd start to smell that Trixton was a trick. And that, my handsome fellow, is why we're going back to see Henry."

"I must say you have a peculiar insecure streak. You're the most ingenious person I've ever met, and yet you're always wanting to run off to your friends for advice."

"Oh, we're not going to Henry for advice this time. We're going to him for makeup."

Artie shrugged noncommittally. "Suit yourself. Personally, I think you look lovely in what you have on."

"Not *me*, silly. *You*."

"Huh?"

"Look, it stands to reason: since Mr. Trixton looks like you ... then you will obviously have to look like someone else."

"What? But that's ridiculous."

"On the contrary, it's eminently sensible." She pulled him toward her again. "Besides ... I think it will be fun, don't you?"

A welcome assault on his lips forestalled any reply.

Eight o'clock the next morning found Artie wedged into the car between Elyse and Mariel. Everything had fallen into place for their strange errand: Lila was not shooting today, leaving Henry free to accommodate them; and Elyse, who said she could not think of any way she'd rather spend her morning (apart from a long list of sex acts), had offered to drive them to Culver City. With the scriptwriting day set to begin at noon in the underutilized back room of the Startled Egret restaurant, they'd have a couple of hours to let Henry work his magic.

"Let's just make sure I don't have to spend a couple of hours every time I get in and out of my new chin, or whatever you have in mind. I don't want to make a part-time job out of transforming my face to and fro."

"No, I guarantee it'll be a quick change both ways. I want your face between my legs after hours, not in front of a mirror."

"If it's any help," said Elyse dreamily, "I can hold the mirror while you go between her legs."

Artie enjoyed that scenario in his mind's eye for a moment. Eventually it was replaced by a much less appealing image: Lubb. He said the name aloud.

"He could unmask me, couldn't he? You know, if he and Heffy compare notes, and Lubb lets out with a what-the-fuck-are-you-talking-about-Sid-there-was-nobody-called-Trixton-here-you-must-mean-Artie-Plask-the-new-writer. Or words to that effect."

"Don't worry about that," Elyse said. "I had a chat with Lubby last night. He knows I would be sad if he said anything like that. Ergo, he won't do it."

Henry seemed, if possible, even more magnanimous than on the previous occasion.

"Hello, hello, hello," he boomed, one *hello* for each of his guests. "Elyse!" He gave her an extra-special greeting, lifting her gently off the floor by her waist and spinning her around. "Lila told me the terrific news," he said when he'd redeposited her on land.

"So," he continued, looking now from Mariel to Artie and back, "what are we doing for Mr. Plask? You said on the phone we need to disguise him as your sponsor?"

"It's the other way around. *This* is how he looked in his cameo appearance as the sponsor. Therefore we have to give the *original* Artie a fresh look."

Henry roared with laughter. "You certainly have a complicated way of doing things."

"What do you recommend, Henry?" Artie asked. "A wig? A mustache? Eyeglasses? False teeth?"

"*Please*," said Mariel. "Not false teeth. And make sure you keep him good-looking, you understand? Whatever monster you create, Elyse and I need to work with him day after day."

"How do you feel about eyebrows?" Henry asked.

"I *adore* bushy eyebrows," Elyse exclaimed. "I love to run my fingers over them." She licked her lips.

"Yes," Mariel concurred. "Eyebrows will be most agreeable."

"Mmm," said Elyse, shifting sensuously in her tight dress.

Henry was making notes on a pad. "Okay: Eyebrows. A wig, certainly – how about that sandy red one?" He pointed toward a shelf. "I think your complexion is pale enough to carry it off. Of course your eyebrows," he continued, gesturing toward Elyse with his own eyebrows, "would have to be that color as well."

"I think that will suit him," said Mariel heartily.

"I think it will suit him, too," Elyse agreed.

"Yes, it'll suit him," said Artie, momentarily caught up in the third-person atmosphere. "Only ..."

"What?" said Mariel.

"I was just thinking about my body hair."

"Peachy!" said Elyse. "May I think about your body hair, too?"

"What I mean is ... I'll have to wear long sleeves all the time – and definitely no swim trunks." He pondered this for another moment. "I guess it's all right. I've never been that sensitive to heat or cold, one way or the other."

"And you can make up for your workaday apparel by showing us plenty of nudity after sundown," said Mariel.

"Which will be duly reciprocated, of course," said Elyse.

Henry fetched the wig and held it up to the light. "I'll trim this so it sits just right on your head. The eyebrows can be affixed with a good-quality gum each morning, and they should hold nicely."

"What else does he need?" Mariel asked.

Henry frowned. "I think mustache disguises are a little crude. Eyebrows are more subtle and yet, believe it or not, more effective at altering the overall personality of the face – so I'm satisfied as far as all that goes. We will give you spectacles, though," he said to Artie.

"Which are much quicker to apply than a mustache," said Mariel.

"And much less likely to fall off into one's food," Artie noted.

"Just don't peer too deeply into your soup," said Elyse.

"If it weren't for the quick-change requirement, I could develop a makeup landscape that would *really* transform your face," Henry said wistfully. "No offense, mind you."

"What you've laid out will serve present purposes beautifully," Mariel assured him. "Let's see how it looks, shall we?"

# Chapter 10

In Hollywood, Artie was learning, projects could stall indefinitely or they could come to fruition instantly. By the end of the day, two networks had offered to put Elyse on the air as soon as she could line up a cast. With Heffy stinking up the airwaves on Saturday nights (as Mariel had put it), Elyse was advised by her friends to sign with the company who could put her on Fridays – which happened to be Sid's own network – rather than the one offering to air her show on Sundays. While being on opposite Heffy would have been ideal, making a big splash the night before would hopefully cast a shadow over his display of serious artistic purpose gone awry.

Also by the end of the day – as momentous a Thursday as Artie had ever known – the initial script for Elyse was nearly complete. As for a cast, Henry had assured them at the end of the makeup conference that he could have any number of actors at their doorstep within minutes of posting an index card on the notice board outside the studio casting office – which he'd promised to do immediately.

The team felt confident enough to tell the network to schedule the first broadcast of *The Metropolitan Mannequin Company Presents the Elyse Heffernan Show* for the following week. While Mariel, Artie, and Elyse held auditions in the back room of the Startled Egret on Friday, Mickey would make the rounds of the press, circulating the release that Mariel had written and announcing a pre-debut photo party for the following Tuesday.

"If things go right, we'll have Elyse on everyone's lips by next weekend," Mariel said with satisfaction as they reviewed the schedule.

"I very much like the sound of that," their star testified.

The script called for the following characters, in addition to the irresistible Louisa Scarsdale (who was to be played, naturally, by Elyse): Giles Pumice, a handsome but absentminded sculptor who occupied the apartment across the hall from Miss Scarsdale; Skynneflynt "Skinny" Codicil, her lawyer; and an unpredictable building handyman called Mr. Stairstep. Louisa, the writers had decided, was a moderately successful fine-art painter of presumably independent means, living an Elyse Heffernan–type existence that would be frequently hinted at in her dialogue with the men who surrounded her.

Stairstep and Skinny were easy to cast, Hollywood boasting a surfeit of extraordinarily gifted character actors. The role of Giles, by contrast, proved more of a challenge. The town had plenty of strikingly handsome faces – and for publicity purposes and the benefit of the studio audience, whoever played Giles had to look the part – but most of the unemployed Adonises who could act well did not specialize in comedy. Artie, peering out at the world through plain-glass spectacles beneath russet eyebrows, was a little nervous when they undertook Saturday's script-revision meeting with the part as yet unfilled.

They'd just begun when a dapper young stranger quietly let himself in from the Egret's main dining room. He moved with an exaggerated but elegant purposefulness as he tiptoed in and eased the door shut.

"Wait a second." Mariel stopped Gabe in mid–punch line. "Who's that?"

His attention drawn to the door by the interruption, Benny smiled apologetically. "Hello, Brian. I don't think we're doing laps today."

It took Artie a split second to parse this, but he succeeded. Elyse, he recalled, had encouraged Benny to invite a gentleman friend to sit on his lap when he wrote lines, Elyse performing this function herself for the others. Benny's beau had been out of town, but he was finally making an entrance today – when Elyse, however, was too involved in trying out the material to lap-hop.

Brian smiled agreeably. "Good thing I'm not wearing my track shorts, then."

It may have been an obvious line, but Brian had come up with it spontaneously and delivered it with perfect timing – and in a velvety baritone whose effect on Elyse and Mariel was immediately apparent in their faces, and likely in their underpants as well. Artie was impressed.

"Are ... you ... an ... actor?" Mariel asked slowly, stepping carefully toward him as if afraid he'd startle like a wild animal and fly back out the door.

The young man laughed. It was a mellifluous laugh that would have been contagious, had all present not been tense with their focus on the conversation. "Good heavens, no," he said modestly. "I'm a doctoral student in linguistics."

"That means he's available," said Benny to Mariel. "Right, sweetie?" he said to Brian. "You'll take a part in our program, won't you?"

The linguist looked around the room with an expression of amused gratitude. "I suppose articulating Standard English over the radio might qualify as fieldwork ..."

"We don't write Standard English," Mickey cautioned. "We write comedy."

"But since you're with Benny, we'll stretch a point," said Mariel hastily. "Please take a seat, Brian."

Benny scarcely had a chance to say *You're playing Giles rehearsal Friday at three show goes on for the East Coast at four thirty* before the door opened again.

"Look at this bunch of cummerbunds."

All eyes went to Sid Heffy – which was, of course, his intention.

"Hello, Daddy. Did you come all the way here just to use that antique line on us?"

Sid's own bulbous eyes continued to roam the room, stopping when they landed on redheaded, bespectacled Artie.

"Who's that clown?"

Artie wondered if Sid had deliberately chosen to call him a clown rather than a cummerbund, or if the insult of the moment had simply been supplied from Heffy mind to Heffy mouth at random. The distinction between a *clown* and a *cummerbund* was probably a narrow one; but to a wordsmith like Artie it held a certain fascination.

"That's Artie Plask," said Mickey nonchalantly. "You know, the writer you fired before even meeting him."

"What a cummerbund."

"Isn't it interesting how you can always tell when a comedian is without a writing team?" Mariel said loudly to Mickey. "The recycled material goes stale so quickly."

"Oh, I have a writing team, all right," Sid bragged. "His name is Lionel Stimpson, and he can write circles around the bunch of you."

"I guess that works well if you want a script that goes in circles," said Mariel.

Heffy ignored her, turning to Elyse. "I really have to take my hat off and hand it to you," he said with sarcastic bitterness.

"That's a malapropism, Daddy."

"You bet it is," said her father proudly, apparently having no inkling what the term meant.

"Actually," said Mariel, "it wasn't a malapropism, exactly. Perhaps catachresis?"

"No, I don't think that's quite right, either," said Brian authoritatively.

Sid, though oblivious to the nuances being explored in the impromptu technical symposium, noticed Brian when he spoke. "And who's *that?*"

"That's a doctoral student in linguistics, naturally," said Elyse. "My, Daddy, you're certainly asking a lot of questions. I thought you weren't interested in my comedy program."

"Comedy? That's a laugh," scoffed Heffy, oblivious to his own unintentional witticism, such as it was. "Your friends here don't know jack beanstalk about comedy." This turn of phrase was another Heffy trademark. "Let me tell you something, little girl: *The Sid Heffy Show* was funny because of Sid Heffy, and Sid Heffy alone. These freeloaders were just along for the ride," he concluded tautologically.

"Now you're being ridiculous," said Mariel over the general hubbub of indignant muttering.

"Ridiculous, eh? *I'll* show you ridiculous." And, making good on the threat, he executed the type of dramatic exit that Lionel Stimpson would presumably have encouraged, looking like nothing so much as a petulant, overgrown duckling whose down had been permanently puffed up by one too many long-winded fan letters.

"And if that's not ridiculous enough," Mariel said after the star had duck-waddled out, "you can tune in to his program tonight."

# Chapter 11

Mariel's diminutive countertop radio set was jade green like Elyse's bathing suit, with coral-pink accents whose hue, in turn, reminded Artie of Elyse's nipples. The radio's fetching streamline contours – not, of course, as impressive as Elyse's personal contours – gave it the appearance of an Art Deco hotel, compressed to a single story and miniaturized.

Crowded into the little hotel this night were the incongruously large ego of Sid Heffy and the sprawling dreariness of Lionel Stimpson. Artie and Mariel had covered her tiny kitchen table with bottled beer and Chinese takeout, to sustain them through the challenge of listening in.

*"Ladies and gentlemen, Dressinger Clothing presents* The Sidney Heffy Dramatic Culture Hour.*"*

Even the announcer – the same announcer whose jollity had set high expectations for week after week of Sid Heffy comedy – sounded pretentious and grim.

*"Thank yow, laydaze and gentilmin,"* drawled Heffy after the respectful applause had died down.

"What the hell was *that?*" shouted Mariel.

"I'm not sure, but I think it was Heffy's idea of an Oxford University accent. As befits the Drama, you know."

*"Toon-eye-it, we givyo the eenisseeal instylmint of a middern misterpease by Ly-oh-nil Stimp-sawn."*

"Oxford University?" said Mariel skeptically. "Oxford University on which planet?"

*"It is our pr'foond h'yope that you will faynd* Niagara Sarcophagus *to be intellekshually unretching."*

Following this mercifully short introduction, a morose orchestra whined for eight measures, after which the nation was treated once again to the voice of Sid Heffy – this time in character.

*"Dark. Another dark night. So dark."*

"It never ceases to impress me how a great radio talent can use a minimum of words to evoke a rich atmosphere," Mariel observed. "He only said *dark* three times, but I swear I can almost picture something dark."

"And, just think," said Artie, "if this were done on a stage, they'd have to spend a fortune dimming the lights, to get the same effect."

*"Never mind the dark, Jim."*

Artie didn't recognize the earnestly squeaky female voice. "Who's the co-star?"

"That sounds like Winnie Liebling. She used to play a pickle vendor from time to time on the old show."

*"So damn dark."*

"Now I get it," said Mariel. "Sid went into drama because it gives him license to say *damn* on the air."

"At least he's dropped the British accent. Somebody must have coached him that the Niagara wasn't Shakespeare's hometown river."

Heffy had been doing okay with the short lines, Artie had to admit – though they were lousy enough in their own right – but as the dialogue became more discursive, the star's limitations became quickly apparent.

*"Inform me, Olivia, inform me why I should stare anywhere but into this dark sky. Paint me a picture of my spleen – paint it and inform me. There was a time when I would have waded in this primordial river ... waded merrily in this river, I tell you. You didn't know me then, Olivia, nor I you. We didn't know each other then."*

Even a Barrymore could not have made the lines sound good; but the fact that Heffy delivered them like a second-grader who had memorized a chunk of the Constitution without grasping any of its meaning resulted in an effect significantly more odious than that of the hypothetical Barrymore version. Words were run together into arbitrary units or separated by mysterious pauses. Familiar terms like *sky* were over-enunciated, while *primordial,* as a specimen of more advanced vocabulary, was quickly swept under the rug, hustled out of sight in a disguise sounding roughly like "pumordimal," but with fewer syllables. Eschewing anything that could pass for a natural or even, failing that, a "dramatic" rhythm, Sid chug-chugged through the speech as if it were a poorly assembled motor car and he its ill-tuned engine. Heffy and his hapless passengers would be lucky to arrive at their destination without a breakdown, Artie reflected.

"Inform me, Artie. Inform me why we should listen to any more of this."

As he could not think of a reason, they switched it off and opened another round of beers.

Mariel took a deep swig. "Hearing Winnie's voice made me a little sad," she confessed. "It made me realize I may never get to write a pickle-vendor scene for Sid Heffy again. I want to write pickle scenes, Artie. Is that too much to ask from life?"

"Maybe we could write a pickle scene together, in private." He stroked her cheek.

She smiled wistfully. "I'm not talking about sex, you cummerbund. Not until I finish my egg foo yong, at least."

"Okay. Then maybe you could bring the pickle character over to Elyse's show."

"Can't. Sid owns the rights to every character we created for his show. If we so much as write in a waitress opposite Elyse, it had better be a waitress with a different attitude and a different accent from any *Heffy Show* waitress who ever took a dessert order, or the bastard will serve us up a blue-plate lawsuit."

"Oh. Well, anyway, if all goes according to your plan, everything will soon be back to normal, right? We'll be scripting comedy for Sid Heffy, Elyse will retire to the form of private life she most enjoys, and I can stop running around in a wig and glasses. And you can write as many pickle-vendor scenes as the market will bear."

"I guess I'm having a temporary lapse of confidence." Suddenly, she seemed to be on the verge of tears.

Artie held her. "It's just the effect of that awful program. That was enough to depress anyone. Even you."

She looked up at his face. "You say 'even you' as if I were something special." Then she smiled again, her eyes still glimmering with traces of moisture. "All right, I suppose I am. But I don't usually think of it that way."

"That's because you never slow down long enough to get a good look at yourself. But I'm getting a good look at you now, Mariel Fenton. In fact, there's no such thing as a *bad* look at you."

Her discouraged mood seemed to pass; nonetheless, the beer had obviously had a mellowing effect, and Artie savored the languid presence of her body in his arms. She tasted like the sweet condiment they'd had with their dumplings, with tipsy hints of lager murmuring to him of relaxed muscles and slow, lazy sex.

"You feel nice," she said. It was a mild statement on the face of it, but she sounded so wonderfully content.

He began undoing her blouse, letting his fingers linger sleepily on every button. He kissed the plump hilltops of her breasts, squeezing them from below in an affectionate rhythm. His instinct tonight was to soothe her and arouse her at the same time, to cuddle her soft bosoms, for example, into flame-tipped erogenous mountains, and nuzzle her cozy pussy into dripping desire.

She spread her legs slightly when he unfastened her bra, and her shoulders arched against the humble support of her kitchen-table chair. He licked one nipple, over and over, challenging himself to do it as unhurriedly as possible. Her moans seemed to come from her throat, not her mouth, as if her body didn't want or need to make the effort of projecting her voice outward.

For a moment, he struggled with the awkwardness of caressing an inner thigh under the table, the circumstances preventing him from getting much beyond Mariel's knee. "I have to get you in bed," he reported.

"No, not bed," she answered. "The bath. I want a bath tonight."

He enjoyed stripping her of her skirt while they stood in front of the tub, and watching it glide down to the floor. She turned in profile to him as she bent to unhitch her stockings, steadying herself on the vanity, and he admired the self-possessed convexity of her bottom in its cream-smooth tap pants.

While she was occupied with the garters, he stepped behind her and clasped her waist, dipping down to nudge the underside of a cheek with his cock-bolstered trouser front. The sound of the bathtub as it gradually filled suggested thick, twisting currents of percolating lust.

Together they completed her undressing. Artie observed how softly naked Mariel looked tonight – more naked, because she was more relaxed.

The tub was finally ready, and Mariel got in, showing the smile of her pussy when she stepped over the threshold.

"Is there room for me?" Artie asked.

"Of course," she said.

He took his time shedding his clothes, though his cock was hard and his nerves sizzling with eagerness for her body. He was relishing the sight of spritely woman in repose in her bath – as a painter might have titled the scene. Mariel's skin was already pinkening, as if the caress of the bathwater had an arousing effect on her flesh.

It took some skill for him to add his own body to the exhibition; but once he got every limb in place, he found the situation surprisingly comfortable. Mariel was obviously happy with it as well – she wriggled on her bottom and murmured a heartfelt *mmmm*.

Then she claimed a fat, fluffy washcloth from the rim, handing it to Artie. He saw that it was the type sewn up like a mitten.

"Do something with that, will you?"

She closed her eyes, simultaneously taking the weight of Artie's dick in her hand – their position here, knees up and face to face, making this maneuver as natural as could be. Her cunt, contrasting so marvelously with his cock in anatomy but positioned quite symmetrically within his reach, clearly awaited him.

He donned the pale blue mitten, submerged it and saturated it, and delivered it to the doorstep of her need.

Her soapy grip delighted his shaft while he rubbed her lips delicately with the pleasure-mitten. She responded to him by shrugging her torso backward a bit, opening her groin wider to him. Her breasts invited his kisses.

The masturbation she was supplying was almost relegated to the background of his consciousness as he focused on driving her toward ecstasy with the wet, warm fabric. Mariel was keeping her body passive now, letting him gradually excite her … twitching minutely and whimpering faintly as his strokes, circles, and squeegeeing motions subtly stimulated her.

Finally she shifted her weight forward to take charge of her pleasure, trapping Artie's washcloth hand under her crotch. She clasped his wrist and rode the mitten, kissing it lewdly with her slit, her clitoris, the undercrack of her ass – writhing all over the cloth, invisibly adding her own moisture to its texture. Still she worked Artie's cock, which was beginning to vibrate in her grip.

He managed to pace himself, and an emotional warmth coursed through him when Mariel cried "Oh fuck oh fuck" and humped his hand in a frenzy. Her eyes popped wide open as the orgasm crested.

"Here," she said quickly, as soon as she could speak again. She peeled the washcloth from Artie's paw and inserted her left hand. In another instant she'd shoved it under his balls.

The solid comfort of this cushion under his sack and the tickle on his perineum made him wild, and soon his cock was sobbing gratefully into his lover's wet, clenching palm. A gurgling, abandoned sound came out of his mouth, making Mariel's eyes brilliant with approval.

# Chapter 12

The casting of Brian as Giles Pumice had been the final essential detail in turning *The Elyse Heffernan Show* from a scheme in Mariel's mind into an on-the-air reality. On Tuesday, the ensemble, sparkling with energy, had given the press a top-notch array of slightly risqué photos in which Elyse horsed around with the three male actors. By Friday morning, Hollywood (and presumably the nation) was poised eagerly to hear what Louisa Scarsdale would do to entertain and titillate that evening. And Sid Heffy's foray into the jungle of radio drama, which had been the subject of a fair amount of unenthusiastic discussion in the Monday papers, was, by the end of the week, the nearly forgotten embarrassment Mariel had hoped it would be – at least until the next show.

At breakfast in the main dining room of the Startled Egret – where Elyse, accompanied by an effusive Mariel and a disguised Artie, had specifically planted herself in order to be seen – acquaintances were practically lining up to wish the new star well and assure her of the degree of certainty with which they planned to tune in.

"At this rate, she'll never be able to finish her eggs," Artie said to Mariel, while Elyse listened politely to a noisy monologue from a sound-effects specialist.

"She didn't come here to finish eggs. I don't think she normally eats breakfast at all."

"Really? I would think she'd need plenty of fuel, with all the exercise she takes. The swimming, too."

"I think the Elyse physiology has a special way of converting sex hormones into energy – without diminishing the volume of the sex hormones in the slightest. It's like a cross between photosynthesis and perpetual-motion machines."

Apart from a few frowns from the stopwatch-obsessed director supplied by the network's originating affiliate station, Friday afternoon's rehearsal went reasonably well for a brand-new show with a brand-new star. Artie found himself boyishly excited as the dialogue reverberated onstage, the orchestra practiced its links, and ushers readied the house for the arrival of the studio audience.

Said audience, it had been decided, would be composed of men and women twenty-one or older, as a precaution against any stray innuendos that might disentangle themselves from the innocence-draped raciness of the script and fly around the auditorium.

"Say, what if Heffy decides to drop by?" redheaded Artie said to Mariel. "He'll be expecting to find Mr. Trixton here, won't he? Remember, we told him that he – I – was so interested in the show that he – I – insisted on attending that writers' meeting. Surely such an eager sponsor wouldn't miss his chance to be present for the initial broadcast?"

"That's what I meant about killing him off – so to speak and no offense. If the question is raised, we'll tell Heffy that Trixton had to go back east. To buy more black bathing suits."

But Heffy did not drop by. Meanwhile, the interests of the elusive Mr. Trixton were well represented by the Metropolitan Mannequin Company tagline, along with the midshow commercial Mariel had scripted for the announcer – a sixty-second spot that insisted in fifteen different ways that Metropolitan's mannequins were, in short, better than other mannequins, for reasons best understood by "America's most discriminating department stores." The belabored vapidness of the commercial, and its unsubstantiated puffery, resembled the contents of real ads for real companies so convincingly that Artie found it a bit unsettling.

"I had such fun," Mariel confessed proudly, when he complimented her on the work's nauseating authenticity. Above and beyond the pleasant diversion of crafting fatuous advertisements, she was clearly as excited about today as he was.

As for their star, she appeared as serene in her vitality as ever. Either stage fright was completely alien to Elyse, or she simply had enough recent orgasms in her system to be emboldened against jitters the way some performers were emboldened by that little pre-show drink. She had, Artie noted, arrived at the station with Gabe, who looked as postcoitally salubrious as all of them did after a session with Miss Heffernan. Gabe's elfin ears were pink, and his eyes steamed behind spectacles like mussels in white-wine sauce.

When the audience had filed in and filled every available seat, the actor who played Stairstep walked to the microphone. Seasoned comedian Spokes Malloy had welcomed this side job of warming up the crowd before the show, and within seconds he had them chuckling.

A few minutes later, at a signal from the director, Spokes wound things up and stood aside to make way for the announcer. An "on the air" sign lit up, and the announcer opened the broadcast.

"Ladies and gentlemen, the Metropolitan Mannequin Company presents *The Elyse Heffernan Show*, starring radio's newest sensation, Elyse Heffernan. With James Cavendish, Spokes Malloy, and Brian Remington. I'm your announcer, Leonard Brown, and I'm here to remind you about Metropolitan Mannequins: magnificent mannequins for the modern world."

"Speaking of our sponsor – our *real* sponsor," Artie whispered to Mariel, "why isn't Lila here?"

"You're forgetting how reclusive she is. But I'm sure she'll be listening later from home, when we do the West Coast broadcast."

"What about Mickey? I haven't seen him since the rehearsal."

"I'm sure he's around somewhere. Probably just keeping a low profile."

The orchestra played while the remaining cast entered, scripts in hand, from behind a rear-of-stage curtain, taking their places around the microphone with Spokes and Leonard. After the enthusiastic applause died down, the band cut and a telephone sound effect rang crisply from the wings.

"Hello?" said Elyse. The audience briefly applauded her first word. "Yes, this is Louisa Scarsdale."

"Miss Scarsdale, this is your attorney, Mr. Skynneflynt," said Cavendish in an ingratiating purr.

"Oh, hello, Skinny!" said Elyse seductively.

Cavendish giggled like a ticklish leopard. This was something of a trademark for him, and the writers had lost no time in giving him the opportunity to exploit it. And the audience approved. Most of them probably didn't recognize his name, but they'd seen his face in the movies and definitely knew his laugh.

"Now, Miss Scarsdale, I have a great deal of unfinished business on my desk."

"Well, I – "

She was interrupted by a doorbell sound effect.

"Just a minute. There's someone at the door. Come *innnnnnn!*"

The audience laughed knowingly at the boudoiresque tones in which Elyse articulated the invitation.

Spokes leaned in toward the mike. "G'morning, Miss Scarsdale."

"Hello, Stairstep," Elyse said brightly. "I'll be with you in a minute. My friend Skinny is on the phone, and I need to help him with his unfinished business."

Spokes waited a beat before delivering his line, giving the audience a chance to absorb the double entendre.

"Yes, ma'am," he said dubiously. Laughter rumbled through the studio.

The writers had determined, after a twenty-minute debate in the back room of the Egret, that though Stairstep would more realistically address Louisa as "miss," he'd sound funnier saying "ma'am."

"It's lying all over his desk, you know."

The rhythm was repeated.

"I'm sure it is, ma'am," Spokes said, his voice having acquired a comical quaver – one of *his* trademarks.

The audience was howling.

Part of what made it work so freshly and marvelously, Artie noted with pride, was the fact that Elyse didn't read the lines like a stereotypical ingénue – as if oblivious to the risqué overtones. No, just as Mariel had planned, Elyse sounded sly, like Louisa was in on the jokes – yet she was subtle enough not to milk them or descend to laughing along with the spectators. She simply served up the red-hot material at speed with a sharp, sparkly awareness, like a high-class Continental burlesque artist flashing her panties in the course of some graceful exotic dance.

Sid Heffy might have been the most pompous buffoon ever to play the Palace, but he was right about one thing: his daughter had theatrical talent.

The show was divided into two acts, with Leonard's mannequin commercial and an orchestra number in the middle. During this break the cast retired to the wings, where the writers expressed delight at how things were going.

Elyse took Mariel and Artie into a corner of the backstage area. Steadying herself on Artie's shoulder, she reached under her gown, did a panty-removing shuffle, and presented him with the article that had accompanied her pussy through Act One.

"That's better. I felt a bit constrained. Will you keep those for me?"

"Of course. I'll just slip them into the safe-deposit box here," he said, indicating his jacket pocket. The panties were warm from her body and carried an exciting aroma of sex-goddess perspiration and honey.

During Act Two, he watched Elyse's thighs shift under her gown while she gave full value to her lines.

"Look," Mariel whispered. "She's masturbating."

"Yes," said Artie, "I noticed."

"Hands free, and so discreetly that most of the audience won't catch on."

"She's a virtuoso," Artie acknowledged. "Do you think she'll come during the program?"

"My bet is she keeps herself on the edge till we go off the air."

"I can hardly waiiiiit," Elyse was saying with gusto, as Louisa endorsed Stairstep's plan to give her kitchen a new coat of paint. "When can you do it?"

"Well, ma'am, today's a busy one. But I could paint you on Thursday."

"Excellent, Stairstep," Elyse cooed. "*You* come Thursday, and *I'll* be primed."

"I think I'm going to have an orgasm before she does," Mariel confessed, while the audience roared.

"Thanks for the compliment," said Artie. "As you may recall, I wrote that line."

At the end of the show, the front-of-stage curtain closed. While the audience applauded with vigor, the cast dispersed for the intershow break; only Elyse remained onstage.

"I wonder what she's doing," said Artie. The cast and crew had vacated the wings as well for the time being, leaving Artie and Mariel alone there.

Elyse, script still in hand, was backing toward the rear-of-stage curtain. She glanced behind her momentarily when she reached the wall, verifying that she was aligned with the invisible boundary where the two halves of the curtain met. Then she dropped the script and faced forward again, putting her hands on her knees and pointing her ass backward.

"Sexy," mumbled Artie.

Mariel's hand had entered his trousers at the waist. Now she hooked her fingers down into his briefs, and his cock, making its initial curve toward his latest erection, swept up to meet them, playing host to the guests in his underwear.

"Look!" Mariel said suddenly.

A figure was emerging from behind the curtain – Mickey.

As had clearly been arranged beforehand, he seated himself under Elyse, who widened her stance to make room for him. While Artie and Mariel looked on with interest, Mickey reached up to finger the star's pussy – a pussy that they knew, courtesy of the fragrant evidence still in Artie's pocket, to be gloriously naked beneath the skirt.

After a minute, Mickey scooted down further, pulling Elyse downward with him so that she straddled his face in a close thigh hug.

"See," whispered Mariel, "I told you he was keeping a low profile."

The face of Elyse Heffernan being tongued to orgasm by the head-giving head writer had to be the most compelling thing that had ever appeared on this stage, thought Artie. Elyse, one could tell, approached every climax with the control and self-assurance with which a painter approached a blank canvas. The artistic mastery expressed in her face was overlaid with sensory pleasure, burgeoning arousal, and erotic anticipation – hers was the fiery-eyed face of a genius watching her creation come to life, exactly as she had envisioned it.

As Artie watched the star's tongue glide over her lipstick and her nostrils flare with stately sensuality and her cheeks flush the prettiest nipple pink, his cock danced in Mariel's grip. And though the portrait of ecstatic womanhood he was studying was a portrait of Elyse, the aroma of aroused womanhood enveloping him was the aroma of Mariel. And when he and Elyse came, together but separately, his orgasm pointed toward one thing: making Mariel come just as hard.

She withdrew her hand from Artie's shorts and wiped it dry on the fabric.

"Come on," he said, wrapping his own hand around the still-slightly-sticky feminine fingers.

He led her into the corridor and toward a small office that Mickey had shown him earlier, which, though unoccupied after business hours, was left unlocked in case anyone needed pads, pencils, and the like.

"Need any pads or pencils?" asked Artie, after they'd locked the door.

"I need a pencil, all right," said Mariel. "A big, fat, jumbo pencil right up my – "

Before she could even finish the line, he had her bent over a desk. "Hold that thought – and that position," he said. Then he crouched down to slide her panties off, kissing her liberally on her stockinged calves while he lifted one Mariel foot, then the other, to remove her pussy-painted underpants.

"'Lyse left, Marry right," he said to himself mnemonically, situating Mariel's panties in the jacket pocket not occupied by those of their friend. Then he moved on to the trouser pocket that held the nearest rubber.

She wiggled her derriere; he lifted her skirt and stroked her pouting lips, feeling how ready she was. She turned her head to watch him, her mouth open with want, as he outfitted himself with the condom. Then he braced himself on her hip and plunged in, letting her feel every bit of him sinking into her tunnel. He groped her adorable ass while they fucked.

"I ... love ... you," he chanted, riding the rhythm of his own thrusts.

"Ohhhhhhhh," was all Mariel could manage. But he knew what she meant.

He bounced against her bottom. He fingered her lips where they ringed his cock, then spread her juices to her clit. The stiff little button became his entire focus, and he swirled the honey onto, over, under, and around it until he felt her cunt clenching in what could only be the uncontrolled spasms of climaxing woman. He danced with Mariel, pelvis to ass-cheeks, to wallow along with her, his modest dose of second-round spunk stuttering into the rubber deep inside her.

Their breathing filled the soundscape of the little office for several minutes as they recovered from the romp.

"What do you say we get a bite to eat?" Mariel suggested after a while. "We still have a couple of hours before the West Coast broadcast. I can't wait to do everything all over again!"

"Every bit of it?" grinned Artie.

"Every bit of it," answered Mariel.

# Chapter 13

The call from Mickey came first thing in the morning, rousing both of them in Mariel's bed. Artie, who was closer to the instrument, offered to pick up.

"Hello?"

"Oh, hi," said Mickey. "Who's this – Artie?"

"Probably. Unless I'm supposed to be Mr. Trixton again."

"Well, we did it, kid," Mickey tooted. "Sid just phoned me, and he wants us all back on staff right away. With raises all around, which I guess is his way of apologizing for all the insults."

"So it worked like a charm, eh?" said Artie, turning to share his smile with Mariel.

"Almost," said Mickey. "There is one complication."

"Oh? What's that?"

"He not only wants Elyse's writers back ... he also wants her sponsor."

"Sponsor? But the sponsor is as fake as my russet eyebrows. *You* know that."

"I said it was a complication, didn't I? Apparently while we were busy eclipsing Heffy, Lentilla Dressinger was discovering a previously unknown passion for astronomy that has now eclipsed her interest in culture. The money that previously put *The Sid Heffy Show* on the air will now be used to endow observatories instead."

"I see."

"So put on your russet eyebrows – or whatever outfit you brainstorm best in – and fill Mariel in on all this, will you? I figure since the two of you got us this far, you're in the best position to come up with the next step. I told Sid I'd have to get back to him."

Mariel seemed more intrigued than troubled by the situation. She phoned Elyse, suggesting the new star pick them up for a breakfast meeting. Elyse, cooperative as always, assured Mariel she'd hop in the car right after her next orgasm.

"The way I see it," said Artie over his pancakes, "we just have to tell Sid he'll need to find a new sponsor. We can blame it on Mr. Trixton, who will never forget the way Sid insulted him that day at the pool." He raised his fork in simulated indignation, pantomiming his alter ego's wounded sensibilities.

"Precisely," said Mariel, munching toast. "And as soon as word gets out that Sid's going back to comedy, he ought to have his pick of sponsors."

"And what happens to me?" said Elyse.

"Exactly what you wanted," said Mariel. "You return to your life around the swimming pool – and the bedrooms, bathrooms, and billiard rooms of the Heffy mansion – with your coterie of humorously inclined lovers."

"Being a radio star makes my panties moist," Elyse reflected.

"Almost *everything* makes your panties moist," Mariel observed gently.

"Couldn't we keep my show as well?"

This seemed to take Mariel by surprise. She frowned thoughtfully. "That's a good question. Remember, your program was financed by Lila, with the understanding that it was a short-term arrangement, just until we made our point and brought your father back into the fold. I doubt Lila would be willing to subsidize us indefinitely, no matter how much her eyes light up when we mention your name."

"No, I can see that," said Elyse. "But couldn't I get a new sponsor, like Daddy's going to?"

"I'm not sure," said Mariel. "It won't be as easy in your case. Our initial glorious success may have been enough to scare the baggy pants off Sid Heffy, but a business – a real one, that is, not a fictitious outfit like Met Mannequins – may be unlikely to throw in its lot with a brand new show that stars a brand new talent. Real sponsors like a formula that's proved itself over a period of time, in one medium or another. But let me think this over, and see what kind of angle I can come up with."

After breakfast, Elyse asked if they wouldn't mind stopping by her favorite clothing shop. While the goddess wandered the aisles, the writers found their attention drawn to a cranky store manager who was seated on the floor, in an almost lewd embrace with a mannequin who had toppled over. Even the mannequin looked sullen.

"Piece of junk," the man was muttering. "Why can't anyone make these things better? I'd pay double."

Mariel and Artie shook their heads and strolled away, drifting through the open door to the sunlit sidewalk.

"It's a shame we're not really in the mannequin business," joked Artie.

All of a sudden, Mariel's fingers were grasping his forearm. Her eyes were as intense as he'd ever seen them. Even her cloche feather seemed to strut with inspiration, an illusion delivered courtesy of a mild breeze.

"Artie," she began firmly. "Do you know who's going to sponsor Elyse?"

He was, of course, eager to find out. "Who?"

"The Metropolitan Mannequin Company."

He broke into laughter. "What? What are you talking about? It doesn't really exist."

"It will now. You heard the man." She gestured back into the shop, where the put-upon manager continued to hold the floor with his wrestling act. "All we need is a little capital to set things up, and soon this poor man and his brethren will know that if a mannequin says 'Metropolitan' on it – because *ours* will be proudly labeled ... I'm thinking on the right ass cheek, unless you prefer the left – then it's a better mannequin. And that no quality clothing store, large or small, would dare be seen dressing anything else."

Not for the first time, and presumably not for the last, Artie found that strategizing with Mariel put him slightly off balance. *But what of it?* he thought. Equilibrium was overrated.

"What an idea!" he replied. She certainly made the scheme sound plausible. "But, listen, what bank is going to loan us mannequin mad money in this depression?"

"Who said anything about a bank? We're going to borrow it from Lila."

"But you said – "

"I said she wouldn't want to keep subsidizing us. This is an *investment*. We use half of it – roughly speaking – to establish our mannequin biz, and the other half to keep Elyse on the air. Pretty soon Met Mannequins will be profitable, and Lila gets everything back, with interest. Plus she gets to hear Elyse sizzling through her radio every Friday night for the foreseeable future."

"You're incredible."

She bowed her head to accept the compliment. "Your contributions will be instrumental, of course, every step of the way. Do you know how to write business materials?"

"I haven't spent a decade writing comedy for nothing," he replied. "But where are we going to make these mannequins?"

"I'm glad you asked. I have an uncle in Santa Barbara, who for years operated a toy factory. He's retired now – and bored as hell – and his factory is sitting idle. Uncle Mert will be thrilled to get involved in this. It's perfect – I've been meaning to get up to Santa Barbara anyway, to get my ass rubbed by Sheridan."

"To get your ass ... *rubbed?*"

"You bet. Sheridan is a special friend of mine, who knows a thing or two about massage. Whenever I literally put my ass in his hands for half an hour, I get a new lease on life ... and he gets a wet spot on his massage table. I think I'll go up tomorrow. Will you join me? We can start coming up with material for next week's show on the train."

"You mean next week's *shows*, plural. Don't forget, you now have us juggling two different programs *and* setting ourselves up in the mannequin trade."

"It does sound like a lot, doesn't it? But don't worry. After one of Sheridan's ass rubs, anything is possible."

"But *I'm* not planning on getting an ass rub."

"No, but you'll be watching while I get mine. Now, let's go back in there and get things rolling."

Artie tagged along as Mariel made her way toward the mannequin-burdened manager. En route, she caught Elyse's eye and beckoned her over.

"Excuse me, sir," said Mariel. "I'd like to introduce Mr. Trixton from the Metropolitan Mannequin Company."

The man disentangled himself and stood up. "Metropolitan Mannequins? I don't think I ..."

"You know," Mariel continued, "the ones who sponsor Miss Heffernan here on the radio."

The manager turned to look at Elyse. "Ohhhhh," he said, with interest.

"Our newest line of *high-quality* mannequins will be ready for shipment in just a few weeks. May we have one of our salesmen call on you?"

"Oh, yes, please do. Here ..." He fumbled in his vest pocket. "Here's my card."

"What's the reputation of that clothing shop, Elyse?" said Mariel as they drove on.

"A lot of fashionable women seem to like it. You see things there first, before they spread to the other stores."

"Perfect," said Mariel.

"Mariel has decided that we're going to sell the world a better mannequin, starting right here in Hollywood."

"Yes," said Mariel. "It's our way of saying, '*The Elyse Heffernan Show* lives!'"

Elyse, who was sitting in the middle, kissed each of them on the nearest cheek.

"Lila will be supplying the capital," Mariel added.

"Why, that's wonderful!" said Elyse. "Please tell her how grateful I am."

"You can tell her yourself – we're heading to her place next."

"Marvelous!" Elyse gushed. "When did she agree to do this?"

"Oh, about thirty minutes from now," said Mariel. "Depending on traffic."

# Chapter 14

Nanette opened the door when they knocked, looking delicious in a kimono and dark lipstick. Artie saw her face jump from friendly, casual hospitality to nervous, delighted surprise when it registered that Elyse was with them. He surmised that Lila might not be the only woman in the house who found Elyse irresistibly captivating.

"Well, hello!" Nanette said. In her excitement, her words came out in a staccato avalanche. "Please come in. I'll tell Lila you're here. I left her in the bath twenty minutes ago. Goodness, we'd already been in the tub half an hour at that point. Even Lila must be ready to come out by now. Don't you agree?"

While she retreated to the back of the house in search of her lover, Mariel led the others, single file, through the claustrophobic mini-maze of bookshelf-lined hallways, into what Artie thought of as the checkerboard room.

Soon Nanette returned with a similarly kimono-clad Lila. Though in this attire there was something of the onscreen Lila Lowell about her, her diffident manner reminded Artie once again that the onscreen Lila was a performance, not a person. She smiled at Mariel and Artie, in turn, in lieu of uttering any greeting; and she seemed almost unable to look directly at Elyse, though Artie could appreciate how strongly she must have desired to. Nanette, however, was picking up the slack by devouring the goddess unabashedly with her eyes. In other words, the household's collective interest in Elyse Heffernan was well represented.

Since the room did not hold enough seats for all of them, Artie and Mariel stood, leaving Elyse and Nanette to face each other across an unplayed checker game, with Lila at Nanette's side in the third chair.

Lila's business-fluent mind was quick to follow the ins and outs of the current state of affairs regarding *The Sid Heffy Show*, *The Elyse Heffernan Show*, and the Metropolitan Mannequin Company.

"Your uncle can really do it?" Lila whispered, at the end of Mariel's narrative.

Much to his surprise, Artie saw something unusual appear on Mariel's face: a degree of doubt. "I ... think so."

But Lila seemed satisfied, and she nodded at Nanette.

"We'll wire the money up to Santa Barbara on Monday," said Nanette, taking the cue. "And we'll make sure the sponsorship of your show continues." She addressed the latter remark to Elyse.

"God, you're gorgeous." This she also addressed to Elyse. "Lila thinks so, too."

Lila averted her eyes again.

"Almost *everyone* thinks so," said Artie.

"The show Friday night was fabulous," Nanette continued. "I don't mind telling you we listened to it in bed." She stroked Lila's thigh through her kimono.

Artie watched Elyse's eyes light up, as they did so frequently, with sexual interest. "I'm very glad you told me that. Damn, to think of two such beautiful women in bed, enjoying ... me. *Lila Lowell* and her woman," she continued, as if telling herself an erotic bedtime story, "in bed – after a fashion – with me. Oh, my my my."

She shivered erogenously while she spoke. For his part, Artie found that he had his hand in his pocket, and that he was discreetly tickling his cock to the rhythm of Elyse's voice.

She turned to him now. "Can't you just see them, Artie? Undressed and exquisite in bed, touching each other and listening to me – perhaps visualizing me there with them?"

Artie figured Elyse was about the only person in the world who could say something like that without sounding remotely egotistical. Remarks like this were all in a day's work for a sex goddess.

Nanette made eye contact with Lila, who nodded again. "Would you like to see that, Elyse?" Nanette asked.

"You bet," Artie blurted.

Mariel gently elbowed him, snickering. "The question was not addressed to you."

"Sorry." He blushed. "It's ... er ... a side effect of writing her dialogue."

Lila smiled tolerantly.

"Well, Mariel, we're all good friends here," said Nanette.

Elyse was already squirming in her checkers chair, with a palm situated suggestively at the apex of her legs. "You would let me be there while you loved?"

"You'll just have to bring a chair into the bedroom," said Nanette. She looked inquisitively at Lila, who grinned shyly, and then at Artie. "Okay – three chairs."

"I told you Lila would quickly become comfortable with you," Mariel said to Artie as they carried the furniture down the hall.

When the two women reclined naked on their bed, their appearances were thrown into an aesthetic contrast. Lila, as every moviegoer knew, was tall, black-haired, and thin, with breasts like small scrumptious pastries and a round little bubble of an ass. Nanette, in turn, was blonde, compact, and on the voluptuous side. And although, by her own account, Nanette had left the tub long before Miss Lowell, Artie noticed that she still looked positively ripe from her bath, lusciously warm and rosy, while Lila looked stunningly sepulchral as always.

Their bodies faced each other; their heads, framed by deep purple pillows, faced Elyse, who had stripped to her underwear before posing on a chair at the foot of the bed.

"Isn't it clever," Mariel said to Artie, "how the best entertainment in Hollywood occurs behind closed doors?"

Although enough seats had been provided, they'd chosen to stand to one side, which gave them a fairly good view of the overall landscape – though their position denied them, for the time being, a view of Nanette's backside and Lila's front.

There was such beauty all around Artie. Since arriving here, he had been almost constantly surrounded by beauty. Beautiful women – and beautiful men, too, for that matter, though Artie's response to that was more academic. As an aesthete, Artie was glad to be learning to take beauty for granted, in a positive sense, to be coming to view beauty as a dominant feature of his environment.

And, as a devotee of women, he was very glad to be in a room with two naked lovelies mingling in their bed; a universal sex goddess in underwear on a serviceable throne; and – best of all – a colleague (fully clothed at the moment) who spoke as if she'd always known him, and whose sexual appetite, though somewhat generalized like his own, seemed to settle on him with a particular intimacy and significance.

Just as his did on her.

As Lila and Nanette began fondling each other's breasts, Elyse responded by fondling her own. She did it teasingly, at first, through her brassiere ... but soon she removed the confining garment, hanging it from a bedpost as if to commemorate her connection to the events transpiring on the bed.

Elyse twisted her nipples with graceful vigor, and her proud breasts seemed to float in her hands. She opened her legs, hooking them around the legs of the chair to expose the gusset of her white panties to her hosts – and to Mariel and Artie. As the goddess rocked in her seat, Artie saw a dainty wet spot appear at the front of the knickers.

Lila and Nanette now had their breasts pressed together and their hands busy at midbody: Lila's fingers cajoled Nanette's pussy lips open, while her lover rested one hand on a lanky Lowell hip and used the other to pat out a gentle beat on Lila's left derriere cheek. Nanette was moaning, and Lila's mouth hung open like a wanton flower. Still their eyes remained on Elyse.

Artie turned to monitor Mariel's enjoyment of the tableau, and found that she was already gazing at his face, awaiting his attention – while keeping one eye peripherally abreast of the action.

"Hi," she said, just loud enough for him to hear.

"Hi," he answered.

"I'd like this up my skirt," she confided, taking his hand.

He drew her toward him, aligning the apogee of her skirted ass above the crease in his left trouser leg. His right arm girdled her tummy; his left oriented itself to the skirt hem.

Nanette was working her way down the bed, finally allowing her gaze to leave Elyse so that she could mouth pleasure along the expanse of Lila's swanlike body. Lila was still managing to look toward her masturbating guest, but her eyes grew increasingly unfocused with every inch Nanette kissed downward.

Elyse had a hand in her panties, and its rhythm, complementing that of the hand that remained at her chest, was hypnotic. The spectacle of Elyse, ankles hooked behind the chair legs, creaming her panties as she observed the others, was sublime to Artie.

His hand crept up Mariel's stocking, and he savored the warmth of her thigh. When his fingertips encountered bare flesh, Mariel purred, and her rump jiggled against his erection.

He watched Nanette, whose head was now nestled in her lover's crotch, ably manage Lila's ass-cheeks with her hands, while nurturing her slit with – one assumed – a velvety tongue. Lila writhed slowly, each languorous wiggle capped off by a punctuating twitch of ecstasy-in-progress.

Elyse was whimpering. Her self-diddling grew frantic, and she closed her legs around her hand in order to peel her underpants and send them downward like manna from heaven. They landed at her ankles and she nimbly kicked them off, sending them into the air like a satin dove – which alighted on the bed and then, once again resembling a woman's discarded panties rather than a creature of the air, appeared to sit lewdly to take in whatever happened next.

Elyse opened her legs again, wide as they would go, and let both her hands forage in her hot blond nest, her bare swimmer's moon bobbing on the seat atop invisible waves.

When Artie's hand reached the leg hole of Mariel's panties, she answered the finger on her elastic by unzipping Artie's pants. Her palm found his cock just as he made contact with her pussy lips; and as he teased her open, she took him out *into* the open.

The entire bedroom was squirming on the brink of orgasm. Lila squirmed around Nanette's tongue, and Nanette squirmed as well, her hand splitting her voluptuous derriere cheeks to meet her own pussy. Elyse squirmed with abandon in her chair. Mariel squirmed astride Artie's fingers, her cunt juicing itself around his presence and her clit hovering atop his touch. Artie squirmed in her grasp, grinding his hips in time to her strokes.

The orgasm began quietly in Lila's throat, then spread to Nanette's eyes. It traveled in waves to the foot of the bed, where it resonated in every sinew of Elyse's body, ringing out of her mouth in pear-shaped tones.

From there it scurried up Mariel's legs – triggering a bubbly cauldronful of moans when it kissed her deep inside her skirt – and hopped astride Artie's penis, sparking convulsions.

And thus Artie completed the orgasmic tour, commemorating the entire event with a saxophone-shaped glob of spunk on Lila's floor beams.

# Chapter 15

The Sunday-morning train up the coast was nearly empty. "Where would you like to sit?" asked Mariel.

"You choose," said Artie. "I try to avoid anything that smells like a decision before noon."

Mariel selected their seats, and soon the vehicle was in motion.

"Let's see," said Artie. "Diner car is back that way, I think. Oh, and there's a restroom right up there at the end of this car."

"Ah, so there is."

"So, you know, if you have to pee during the trip ..."

"Check."

"I mean, if you want a nice solid toilet seat to rest your soft, round bottom on while you expose your pussy and piss away to your heart's content, while the train hurtles noisily forward nearly as fast as your stream rushes noisily downward ..."

"Artie, I get the idea!" Mariel affirmed, laughing. "I don't need to hear the whole script."

"Maybe not ... but I do."

"Pervert," she teased.

"You started it. Remember that uncharted waterfall in Collander Park?"

She smiled proudly. "Anyway, I'm glad you're capable of *some* constructive thought before noon."

He adjusted his clothing to accommodate the hard-on he'd given himself; then he relaxed and glanced out the window. "Seems it's shaping up to be another warm, beautiful day."

"Um-hmm."

"And I can tell you, I'm glad to be in short sleeves for a change. Isn't there a way to dispense with that redhead routine at this point?"

"I don't see how. At minimum, you need to retain the disguise when we're in meetings for *Sid's* show. And the reappearance of Mr. Trixton in his capacity of mannequin executive does complicate things. I thought you said you didn't mind the long sleeves."

"I *don't* mind the long sleeves. What I mind is being asked ten times a day by strangers, 'Aren't you awfully hot in those long sleeves?'" This was the collateral phenomenon that Artie, more accustomed to the "live and let live" attitude of the New York variety of stranger, had not anticipated.

"I see your point."

"How on earth are we going to write two different shows every week, anyway? I have to say, Marry, if it were anyone but you proposing we do all the things you're proposing we do, I'd be a bit skeptical. But you're something of a miracle worker, aren't you?"

"Maybe. The important thing is that I know where to find the material from which miracles are made. Lila Lowell. Elyse Heffernan. Artie Plask." She exploited the percussive, consonant-heavy syllable that constituted his surname to poke him affectionately in the gut.

"I like the way you pronounce that," he said, stroking her thigh. He wasn't sure he deserved the status she'd given him as part of her miracle machinery, but he basked in the appreciation.

They necked for a few seconds, Artie's hand feathering over Mariel's bottom cheeks beneath her skirt, until the conductor came through and disrupted their privacy.

"It's very convenient that you also have an Uncle Merle in your miracle bag," said Artie after they'd produced their tickets and the official had moved on, thereby broaching a topic that had been troubling him slightly.

"Yes. Only his name isn't Merle, it's Mert. You'll only make a fool of yourself if you go around 'Merling' Merts."

"Yes, of course. Please un-Merle him for me."

"As for the writing chores ... well, for goodness' sake, we have ten writers. So what if some of them have to miss a session to work on the other show?"

"Or to orchestrate a sales campaign for mannequins."

"Right. Don't tell Sid, but we could probably manage with as few as five writers on any given occasion, if we had to. Though six would allow us to form a human pyramid, should the situation ever call for it."

"You think of everything."

"Then again, a human pyramid might result in a general view up my skirt."

"Which would indeed be a tragedy – for those who missed it. But getting back to Mert ..."

"What about him?"

"You tell *me* what about him," Artie urged her gently. "I detected an uncharacteristic tremor in your sales talk when Lila mentioned him."

Mariel sighed. "You're right, Artie. I'm a tiny bit nervous about Mert."

"Why?"

"It's not that he won't *want* to do this. He'll leap at the chance. And it's not that he's not fully *capable* of doing it ... in theory ..."

"What do you mean by 'in theory'?"

"I mean 'in theory,' where everything goes the way it should and the outcome is just as expected." She sighed again. "As opposed to 'in practice' ..."

"In practice, where ..."

"Where things have a tendency to go wrong." She said it in a Lila-esque whisper, as if afraid to hear herself utter the words.

"Wrong ... for Mert?"

"For Mert," whispered Mariel. Then she reclaimed her natural speaking voice. "Oh, he always managed to keep the toy company afloat – even profitable. He retired before the Crash, and if you weren't paying close attention you'd think of it as a success story – which, in the final analysis, it was. But there was an unsettling pattern with Mert, if you *were* paying close attention. Every success seemed to be built on the ruins of a minor disaster. I'm not talking about the usual false starts and modest losses that are a feature of any business of that type; I'm talking about colorful little fiascos that seemed only to happen where Uncle Mert was concerned. Nothing that hurt anyone or caused a national crisis – just funny miniature catastrophes that would inevitably send Mert back to the drawing board with his tail between his legs."

"For example?"

"For example, there was the twin music box."

"Twin music box?"

"Two music boxes, constructed as a unit, that played companion tunes. As one played, it wound the gears of the other, so the songs would play back to back."

"Very nice."

"Endlessly."

"Oh."

"For some reason they also got progressively louder."

"Ah."

"Then there was – oh, but you get the idea. But look, Mert will be working with *us* on this, and I'm sure – well, let's say *almost* sure – nothing will go wrong."

"Okay."

"Remember, mannequins have no moving parts."

"True."

"I think it will be fine." She brightened. "Honestly, I'm excited about the business end of things."

"That's part of what I love about you: you're excited about *everything*. You're like Elyse, only in your case the perpetually moist panties are worn over the brain."

"Thank you, Artie. That may be the most peculiar compliment I've ever received."

He nodded modestly.

"But, yes, I'm excited. I used to handle some sales tasks for Mert, before Lila hired me as her publicist. It's been years, of course, but it's like riding a bicycle – you can always pick it up again."

"As long as you remember where you left it."

# Chapter 16

Their attention to business matters was interrupted by the arrival of another passenger, a long-necked gent who had, judging from the tumbler in his hand, been traveling in the club car until now.

The man was a smugly literary-looking specimen of about thirty-five; his face seemed to project a gift for oblique creative insights and an extreme satisfaction about same. When Artie briefly made eye contact with him, he was reminded of that telltale self-consciousness in the eyes of a painting that immediately identifies it as a self-portrait – though self-portraits rarely looked this conceited.

The self-portrait selected a seat across the aisle from them.

"Ooh," said Mariel. "Bloody Mary. Don't mind if I do."

"Don't forget we have to work on those scripts," Artie cautioned.

This seemed to attract the condescending interest of the new arrival. "Yes, I know what you mean," he drawled. "I cannot tolerate any alcohol whatsoever in my system when I'm creating."

"So obviously you're not 'creating' at the moment, then," said Mariel amiably.

"No," he answered. "This, my dear, is a vacation. Or, to be more precise: I've been fired. Only temporarily, you understand." He took a sip of his drink. "You people are in radio, I suppose," he said superciliously.

"Yes," said Artie. "We write for – "

Mariel cut him short with a discreet squeeze on his nearest available buttock, evidently favoring this variation on the classic elbow in the ribs. "We write for various people," she said decisively.

"I, of course, am Lionel Stimpson," said the man.

Mariel glanced ever so briefly at Artie, raising an eyebrow as if to say, "See, I had a feeling about this."

Once again impressed with her perspicacity, he wondered if Mariel would consider it prudent for them to avoid giving him their names – just as she had prevented him from stating their professional affiliations – and he wondered how they could accomplish this without being rude. He soon saw it was a moot point, however, as the only name their new acquaintance seemed concerned with was the name Lionel Stimpson.

"You've probably seen me at the back of the playhouse on my opening nights. And, accordingly, it will no doubt surprise you to learn that I, of all people, have recently descended to radio as well."

"That *is* a shock," said Mariel dutifully. "But didn't you say you'd been fired?"

A sly grin crept onto Stimpson's boyishly arrogant features. Despite the fact that this popinjay was undeni-ably a handsome popinjay, the effect, in Artie's opinion, was repulsive.

"It's what a *comedy* writer" – Stimpson said the word with distaste – "would, I believe, call a 'great gag.' And I am bound to admit that it is. Picture this, my friends."

Artie bristled inside at being thus addressed.

"Low comedian Sid Heffy, thanks to the prodigious genius of Lionel Stimpson, becomes the dramatic performer he has always dreamed he could be – an artistic gift to America." Stimpson paused. "Then arrives treachery!"

He said this so dramatically that Artie's head jerked toward the front of the car, as if he expected Treachery to come stalking down the aisle in person, perhaps also with a Bloody Mary in hand.

"Yes, treachery. Treachery, in the beautiful but perfidious form of a daughter. A daughter who steals the very audience from the bosom of her own father. Her own father, my friends."

Artie wondered idly how much time would be saved if Stimpson decided to speak without the benefit of rhetorical repetition.

"So what does the genius do? Does Genius accept defeat and skulk back to his playhouse?" Stimpson paused to chortle and take another sip of his cocktail. "No, Genius does not. Genius chooses to take a temporary furlough, while Sidney Heffy pretends to give up the Drama and return to life as a mere clown. His staff of jokemongers returns, and the daughter – for whom this outcome, for reasons known only to her twisted mind, had been the raison d'être of her patricidal debut – retires to private life. And then ..."

Stimpson paused – dramatically, of course – for a few seconds before he resumed his narrative.

"And then, my friends, Genius returns triumphantly to take Mr. Heffy back in hand, leaving ten Hollywood hacks to peddle their cheap gags elsewhere, as *The Sidney Heffy Dramatic Culture Hour* returns to enlighten the masses – this time on a permanent basis."

Artie and Mariel exchanged a look. "How fascinating," said Mariel evenly. "And this switcheroo was *your* idea?"

The playwright's manner became mild for an instant. "Actually, Mr. Heffy came up with the scheme."

"Why, that skunk," Artie muttered under his breath.

"Such skills those vaudeville performers took away with them!" said Mariel, also sotto voce. "Tap dance, juggling, backstabbing ..."

The train was pulling into Oxnard.

"This is my destination," said Stimpson, downing the rest of his drink. "Remember, my friends: the sublime theater of Lionel Stimpson will return to elevate the airwaves shortly. And I can say with all modesty that you will be dazzled. Dazzled." He made his exit.

"That was 'with all modesty'?" said Artie.

"He meant all the modesty he had on hand. In other words, none."

"So, I guess now we're sunk."

"That's the spirit."

"You feel differently?"

"Very," Mariel replied. "It seems to me Messrs. Heffy and Stimpson are playing high-stakes gin rummy without any cards. Consider the following: First, Mickey has not yet promised our services to Heffy. Second, we've already decided we intend to keep Elyse on the air, whether or not we're also writing for Sid. That's why we're on this train, remember?"

"That, and your ass-rub."

"Third, *The Sidney Heffy Dramatic Culture Hour* stinks – and the longer it runs, the stronger the stench. No one will listen to it, and – more important – no one will sponsor it, now that Dressinger has eloped with her telescope. Q.E.D. Which, in case you're rusty, is Latin for 'so there.'"

"I see what you mean."

"Sure, Sid can easily find sponsorship for his *comedy* show, once your Mr. Trixton has turned him down; but this Lionel Stimpson garbage? Not a chance."

Artie sighed with relief, and Mariel continued.

"Now, realistically, when we tell Sid that Elyse is staying on the air, he is unlikely to take it well – especially since, as we've just learned, his ultimate goal is to return to the Drama, *without* intrafamily competition for the public's attention this time."

"But none of it makes any sense," said Artie. "Sid doesn't have to be in competition with Elyse to be lousy and lose all his listeners, right? He could be in competition with any other program – or dead air, for that matter – and he'd still be every bit as lousy and listenerless."

"True. But it was the competition from his daughter – assisted by his former staff – that really rankled ... and it was the competition from his daughter that he has convinced himself was the only factor responsible for his new program's failure."

"The guy is deluded," said Artie, shaking his head and chuckling. "That drama hour of his was so terrible, it was positively hilarious."

Mariel smiled sardonically. "That's an understatement. I'd say it was – *hey!*" Once again, she had grabbed his arm in the orgasmic throes of inspiration.

"What is it?"

"Think about it. You just said Heffy's attempt at serious drama was so terrible it was hilarious. Henry said something like that too, come to think of it, when he looked into his crystal ball that first day."

"Yeah. So?"

"So ... maybe we can all get we want – Heffy, his writers, Elyse, and the American public."

"How?"

"Through our crafty exploitation of the fact that Sidney Heffy is *hilarious* when he thinks he's being dramatically compelling."

Artie broke into a grin. "Inform me, Mariel. Inform me what you have in mind."

# Chapter 17

"Mannequins? Easy," said Uncle Mert, fidgeting cheerfully with his glasses. "They're just big dolls, right? No moving parts, no gimmicks. I could have the first batch ready in a month."

"That's about what I figured," said Mariel. "Excellent."

Mert beamed, and addressed himself to Artie. "This one always had everything figured."

"She still does."

"Someone would have to get up pretty early in the morning to outsmart her."

"Hell, they don't even make mornings that early," Mariel added, gesturing grandly with make-believe hubris and thereby doing a fair imitation of the body language of Lionel Stimpson.

"And always with the wisecracks. If you heard a boy in town say something witty, you knew he'd been dating Mariel."

"*This* boy comes with his own material, Uncle Mert. Artie is a comedy writer, like me."

"Very nice," said Mert. "Then you understand how her mind works, eh?"

"Yes," said Artie. "Once I catch up with it."

"So, what do you want them to look like, these dolls?"

"Like other mannequins, only a little better," said Mariel. "Their eyes should be a little more vivid. Their mouths a little more sensuous. Their noses a little more ..." She looked at Artie for help.

"Perky?" he offered.

"And they not only have to look better, they have to *be* better. Find out how today's mannequin is made, and make sure yours are better engineered, more manageable, more durable. Just like your toys were always a little better than anyone else's." She patted her uncle's cheek, while shooting only the briefest of guilty glances toward Artie in reference to their conversation on the train.

"Hey, they were *a lot* better," said Mert, with a jovial swagger in his voice.

"Of course, sweetie. I was using 'a little' in the sense that means 'a lot.'"

"Hollywood," Mert grunted dismissively.

"Don't forget the plaque," said Artie.

"The plaque?"

"Yes," said Mariel. "Each mannequin must have an elegant metal plate on her left buttock – "

"I think we decided the right," Artie interjected.

"... on her *right* buttock, bearing the legend 'METRO-POLITAN MANNEQUINS.'"

"Say, that's classy," said Mert.

"Make it look like engraved silver, if you can."

After borrowing the telephone to check in – at some length – with Mickey, and the typewriter to compose a draft agreement for Mert to bring to his lawyer, Mariel concluded the business meeting and proposed an afternoon stroll around town. Mert, however, was so eager to start designing that he encouraged them to go without him. He was even thinking ahead to male mannequins, though his first run would be female mannequins only.

"Just think," said Mariel, as she and Artie promenaded. "In a matter of weeks, customers will be lifting the skirts of mannequins to see if their favorite stores are using the best."

"If only Trixie could see me now."

Mickey marshaled his thoughts as he waited outside the Heffy mansion. He'd become so accustomed to letting Mariel do the heavy thinking on behalf of their group that confronting Heffy alone made him a little nervous. Still, she'd given him the outline of what needed to happen – brilliant, as always, even over a tinny long-distance connection.

Lubb opened the door and gave him the usual look of semiconcealed distaste.

Mickey had never understood the point of a Sid Heffy type minus the talent and material. Even in Sid's intermittent motion-picture career, Lubb was no longer welcome as a stand-in: stand-ins weren't expected to make snide remarks about the cinematographer while holding the star's place under the lights, this privilege being reserved for the star alone.

However, as an existentialistic atheist, Mickey accepted that ultimately there didn't have to *be* any point to Lubb's presence among them.

"Is Sid expecting you?"

"No," said Mickey.

Lubb shrugged dubiously but stood aside so that Mickey could enter.

While he stood in the hall awaiting his host, Elyse came in from the patio, betoweled and dripping.

"Are you here to see me?" she asked brightly.

"I wish I were."

Elyse glanced around to make sure her father was not in the immediate vicinity. Satisfied that they were alone, she made a quick grab at Mickey's crotch.

"Don't leave without dessert." She winked at him and disappeared up the stairs, her hips swaying magnificently in her towel.

A moment later, Heffy appeared from stage right, wearing a broad stage smile. "Well, well!" he boomed, clapping Mickey on the shoulder. "How are you this fine Sunday afternoon?"

"Just fine, thanks," said Mickey quietly, in an attempt to lower the overall decibel level.

"Here to talk business, or is this a social call?"

He thought fleetingly of Elyse. "Business to begin with, if that's all right with you."

"Splendid. Splendid!" said Heffy, reaffirming his chosen decibel level.

It was Mickey's private opinion that the word *splendid* really oughtn't be used as an exclamation at all – certainly not twice in a row, and definitely not above a judiciously moderated conversational tone.

"Let's go into the library. Cocktails, Lubb!" Sid commanded to the air, but at a volume that resulted in the unmistakable sound of glassware being assembled as they passed the kitchen.

Heffy's glad-handed manner gave Mickey confidence. *Damn, he must really want us back*, he reflected. *And then he's planning to throw us out again*, he reminded himself, recalling what Mariel had told him about the conversation with Stimpson.

Lubb entered the library with a tray just as they were settling into their armchairs. "You go ahead," said Sid generously. "As you know, I don't drink."

"I don't drink either," said Mickey.

"Get the hell out of here, Lubb," said Sid. "That man wastes so much of my time," he confided to Mickey after the butler had left.

"Sid, I think we need to have a candid discussion about the future of *The Sid Heffy Show*."

"Yessir," said Heffy. "Candied discussions," he went on approvingly, evidently under the impression that it was a confectionary metaphor. "That's the only kind I have."

"I know your dream is to be a dramatic entertainer."

"Well, sure," said Heffy, lowering his gaze in an ineffective simulation of humility. "A man can have his dreams, right?"

"And I know that as soon as Elyse is off the air and you've reestablished your comedy show, you plan to replace us with Lionel Stimpson once again."

Sid sputtered incoherently – as if the shock had somehow overtaken him in mid-cocktail, despite his abstention. "*WhatthepardonmyFrenchfuck?*" was what finally came out, at roughly twice the volume of "Splendid!" as heard earlier.

"Why, you double-crossing bastard," Sid continued, presumably unaware of the irony carried by that remark. "Did you come over here on a Sunday afternoon just to kiss me off?"

"No," said Mickey calmly. "I came here to help you. To help all of us. Except possibly Lionel Stimpson."

"What the fuck are you talking about?"

"You don't need Stimpson, Sid. If you want to do drama, we can write it for you. We'll write drama for you, and comedy for Elyse."

"Elyse! Listen, I don't wanna hear any more about Elyse being on the radio."

"You're going to, Sid. A lot more. She has a sponsor, a team of writers, and the ear of the public. None of that is changing. It's up to you whether you want to waste your time fighting a fruitless battle against your own daughter's career ... or whether you want to do the show you dream of, enchant your public, and enjoy the prestige of having two radio stars in the family rather than one. Think of it, Sid: a radio *dynasty*." He weighed his words carefully. "Like what the Barrymores are to the stage."

He watched Sid's expression relax into a soft glow of tentative pride. Then the man frowned.

"Why should I pay a whole team of you, when I can just buy plays from Lionel?"

"Because, Sid, Lionel's plays stink." Sid's eyebrows registered indignation, but Mickey quickly pressed on, easing his oratory into the most promising vein. "They're not worthy of you. He makes you look like a shmuck – I say it with all due respect – where we will give you the material your talent deserves. Just like we always have."

Heffy took a minute to reflect on this. "Okay," he finally said. "But not ten writers. You don't need that for drama – it's not like with comedy, where you need everyone brain-storming jokes all the time."

Mickey stifled a chuckle. *Little do you know, Sid.* But would they actually pull this off? He'd learned to trust Mariel's instincts. "I suppose we could *try* it with eight writers," he said doubtfully.

"*Six* writers," Heffy countered.

Mickey did his best to look cornered and incred-ulous, feeling secretly grateful for the bargaining skills he'd developed on the Lower East Side. "Okay," he said, shaking his head in a show of resignation and pessimism. "If you insist on doing it that way: six writers it is." Exactly the number Mariel was expecting him to settle on. And there would be plenty of work to go around on Elyse's program. "We'll need your full cooperation as far as coordinating the work schedules for the two shows, of course. Oh, and did you say something on the phone yesterday about Metropoli-tan Mannequins?"

"Yeah. You think they'd want to sponsor both shows?"

Mickey began his reply with a diplomat's throat-clear. "Yeah. Met Mannequins ... I happened to see their Mr. Trixton at the Egret this morning, while I was having breakfast. Your name came up, and – I'm not sure how to put this – I think he probably ..."

"All right, all right, I get it. What a cummerbund. We'll find another sponsor. Dressinger's contracted for one more month, so I've got time."

"If I might suggest something, Sid: when you pitch it, just say *The Sid Heffy Show.*"

"Why?"

"Well, you're a big star in comedy. So far in drama, you're a – that is, you're not a big star *yet* in that field. So if the sponsor initially thinks they're getting a comedy show, it might make things easier."

"Won't they flip when they find out it's a drama?"

Again Mickey suppressed a chuckle. "Not if it's sensational – right, Sid?" He stood, leaning forward to shake the boss's hand. "I'll phone you tomorrow morning to get your approval on the writing schedule. And now I'd like to pop up and see Elyse. To give her the good news, you know."

He left the study hastily, before Sid could change his mind about anything, and headed up the stairs.

Cracking open Elyse's door, he uttered her name, just loudly enough for it to carry into the room and onto the bed.

"Mmm," she said invitingly.

She was curled up naked in bed, knees in, ass out, a perfectly contained whole. He entered and closed the door.

"I bring good news."

"Give it to me, Mickey," she said, without altering her posture or even looking his way. "Come here and give me the good news, right where I need it."

Before going to her, Mickey allowed himself a moment more to admire her from across the room. His cock thickened as he gazed reverently at her ass.

Her beautiful, bare ass.

# Chapter 18

Her ass. Her beautiful, bare ass.

Artie hadn't known quite what to expect from a visit to Sheridan's massage room, here on the second story of an office building in downtown Santa Barbara, but his attendance was being amply rewarded.

After a glass of the sherry that the specialist had offered upon their arrival, Mariel had undressed behind a screen and wrapped herself in a plush blanket. She had then deposited herself, facedown and with her wine-warm bottom exposed, on the table. Her cheeks glowed under Sheridan's work lights, the plump little curves center stage in what felt to Artie very much like a dramatic presentation.

Sheridan, a thin, blond man with serious eyes and fingers like a concert pianist, rolled up his sleeves.

"Comfortable?" he asked solicitously.

"Oh, yes," Mariel attested. "Very."

"Excellent," said Sheridan. "Then I'll begin."

With a deft, professional motion, he placed both his palms against the swell of Mariel's bottom. The veins on his arms bulged as he applied an even pressure to the two hemispheres – something Artie noticed only in his peripheral vision, as his focus was naturally on the ass, not the arms.

With his thumbs operating independently from his fingertips, the masseur applied a sustained kneading motion. Evidently encouraged by Mariel's moans, the masseur continued in this fashion for a while, using left hand and right to describe symmetrical arcs of pressure that rolled simultaneously outward from the meridian that was Mariel's ass crack.

Benefiting again from his peripheral vision, Artie saw that Mariel's toes were slowly wiggling.

He felt that maybe he should be taking notes.

"Are you ready for the pitter-pats?" Sheridan asked, leaning forward.

"Mmm," his charge answered.

Artie appreciated how apt the masseur's onomatopoeia had been as his gentle hands began showering soft, precise pats all over Mariel's derriere. With the downtown sleepy on a Sunday and thus little noise through the open window, the *pitter-pat*s quietly dominated the auditory environment, while Sheridan's measured breathing and Mariel's intermittent moans provided a subtle counterpoint.

Eventually the pitter-pats accelerated. And, as in a symphonic interplay between percussion and strings, their frenetic stimulation alternated with deep, sensual massage movements whereby Mariel's flesh was at once wrestled and nurtured. Her moans were positively earthy at this point, and Artie could smell her arousal as she presumably – as advertised – moistened the table beneath her.

His cock – his whole lap, it seemed – was achingly hard. He wondered how this treatment would conclude – or did he mean *climax?* And he wished, somehow, he could participate.

Something caught his eye. Beside him, Mariel's clothes waited in a tidy stack – capped, like Mariel herself under normal circumstances, by the cloche. The cloche with the feather.

No sooner had the inspiration hit than the quill was in his hand, his eyes meeting Sheridan's with an unspoken "May I?" as he rose. Turning to look at Mariel, he saw the look of encouragement on her face.

The pink cheeks danced as the feather skimmed and skipped, brushed and stroked. Mariel was so relaxed that instead of giggling, she responded to the titillation with syrupy dollops of lazy chuckles. Artie felt feverish as he passionately tickled her bottom, his dick pulsating with excitement. Meanwhile, Sheridan watched discreetly from the other corner of the table.

Then came the climax Artie had wondered about. Mariel spread her legs and straddled the massage table, sitting up and clutching her blanket to her breast to ride her makeshift horse. She had trapped the feather under her bottom so that the quill end stuck out like a tail and the tickly end, one could assume, pleasured her cunt lips as she ground against the table.

Artie watched with fascination as Mariel orgasmed in this bizarre but erotically compelling pose, her face radiant with silent bliss. As she collapsed back to her previous position, he felt his own quiet orgasm seeping into his pants.

Sheridan spoke. "You know, I've always wanted to grab her feather and do that."

"You should've just asked," Mariel mumbled.

"Say, you – redhead. New guy. Aren't you a little hot in those long sleeves?"

Beneath his false eyebrows, Artie winced. Mariel mouthed a *sorry* his way.

"Don't harass Artie," she said aloud. "For Pete's sake, Sid, I wear a blazer every day, and you've never asked *me* if I was too warm."

"Even Sid knows better than to question *your* judgment," quipped Benny. Heffy frowned as he processed the implications of that statement.

"Why do we have a new guy, anyway, when we're working with a smaller staff?" he asked a minute later.

"I told you before: Plask is the writer we hired just before you fired all of us," said Mickey a bit impatiently.

"And because he and Mariel work especially well together, I want them on both shows."

With that, Mickey removed the current page of script-in-progress from the typewriter, and shook it free of the stray water droplets that had found their way there during Elyse's most recent plunge into the pool. He handed the sheet to Sid. "You wanna try this bit aloud, chief?"

Heffy squinted at the page, cleared his throat, and assumed what he presumably thought was a lofty facial expression – though to Artie it suggested a hasty drawing of an annoyed egg.

Sid began reading. "*There she is, so proud and pretty in her little riding habit. It brunks* – sorry – *it* breaks *my heart that she will never know who her real father is.* Who *is* her real father?" Sid flipped the typed page over, as if expecting to find the answer.

"You are, Sid," said Mickey.

"Oh!" said Heffy. "Oh, I get it. Say, this is good stuff." He turned the sheet back the right way. "Let's see, then a bunch of stage directions ... oh, what's this about applesauce?"

"Put your glasses on," said Mariel. "That says *applause*."

Heffy beamed upon hearing that magic word. "Yeah, my glasses. I think they're upstairs. Anyway, I have a golf game in a little while, so if I'm not needed – "

"You're not," said two or three writers in respectful but confident unison.

Within a quarter of an hour, Sid had left the house, Elyse had shed her bathing suit, and the writers were in a huddle around Mickey and his typewriter, giggling like schoolchildren while they modified the scene.

"I think that's about right, don't you?" asked Mariel. "The listeners will think Sid is deliberately cutting up, but it's all sneaky enough that the great and dunderheaded Sidney Heffy can still believe he's doing a twenty-minute dramatic masterpiece."

"Good thing we convinced him to dispense with the studio audience," Mickey noted. "Their laughter might have given the game away." He handed the revised typescript to Artie. "Read that last sentence out, kid, will you?"

Artie cleared his throat, and did his best impression of Heffy's demeanor. "*There she is, so proud and pretty in her deep-sea-diving suit. It breaks my heart that she will never know who her real barber is.*"

Mariel hugged him. "Oh, Heffy, you're so *dramatic!*"

# Chapter 19

The angle of the morning sunlight had advanced to the stage where it began eroding the shadowed portion of the bed, and Mariel's eyes opened.

Artie smiled at her, then continued writing in his notebook. She purred a "good morning," placing a hand on his bare chest.

"Good morning," he replied.

"Which show are you working on?"

"Neither."

"Oh. New sales copy for the mannequins?" In the four weeks since getting things rolling with Mert, they'd used every minute that wasn't devoted to scriptwriting or sex to generate advance mannequin orders in the greater Los Angeles area. And now that the first Metropolitan mannequins were beginning to arrive in stores, they intended to make another tour of the city to get more establishments on board.

"Nope. I'm making a list."

"A list? Of what?"

"Of the balls we have in the air."

"Are you growing nostalgic for the time when life was just a simple matter of writing – and group nudity – around a swimming pool?"

Artie chuckled. "That one day, you mean?"

"Oh, that's right – I keep forgetting you haven't been here all along."

He took it as a compliment. "Here's what I have on my list so far: (1) A radio show in which the star, an irascible and conceited Hollywood legend, is doing comedy when he thinks he's doing drama – and he mustn't find out. (2) A second radio show – whose star, though a dream of an employer in and of herself, is viewed with suspicion by star #1 because she is an intrafamily rival. (3) A fledgling mannequin-manufacturing company that we've promised will show a profit shortly, and with whom my personal appearance is so closely identified in the suspicious mind of radio star #1 that I am forced to wear a disguise in his presence – because he mustn't find out that the mannequin executive who stood up to him is really one of his own writers."

Mariel yawned. "He also mustn't find out that in the interim, radio star #2 has been backed by Lila Lowell. Is that on your list?"

"No." Artie scribbled busily to incorporate this amendment into his work. "Yeah, I can understand why Lila wouldn't want to provoke the sputtering indignation of a guy like Sid, with spittle and malapropisms flying everywhere."

"Lila already *has* provoked it – not intentionally, of course. Didn't I tell you that story?"

He shook his head.

"Three or four years ago, Lila said something that offended Sid, and he still holds it against her."

"*Lila* said something? Lila Lowell, the talkies' only silent cinema star? She hardly ever says *anything*."

"She said it in a movie. Which, of course, means she wasn't really responsible, as she doesn't usually write her own dialogue. But from Sid's point of view, the fact that she said it not just to a roomful of Hollywood insiders, but to America as a whole, made it worse."

"What in the world was the line?"

"Well, it was a rather risqué boudoir scenario – you know what her movies are like – but they were playing it for laughs. So you're all set to see a steamy love scene, but it turns out the beau is a clumsy oaf, and in between the passionate dialogue he's fumbling with his pajama buttons, stumbling over the slippers she's kicked off, and so on. And finally Lila looks at the camera and says, 'O, ye fates' – you know, in that flat, sardonic tone she does so well – 'O, ye fates, I'm desperate for a night of love, and instead I get Sid Heffy.'"

"It's a good gag," said Artie appreciatively.

"Yes, it is. And many a comedian would have been proud of such a reference – for crying out loud, they're making an *archetype* of him. Not to mention it's free publicity. But, no, the great man has to take offense, because perish the thought that anyone should say 'Sid Heffy' and 'O, ye fates' in the same breath ... or imply that there are contexts, such as a boudoir, in which his signature buffoonery would not be welcome."

"Yes, I can picture the whole thing."

"And there you have the ridiculous but authoritative explanation as to why Sid would hit the ceiling if he knew his daughter was being bankrolled by Lila Lowell. He might even throw Elyse out of the house, and then where would we be?"

"At the Startled Egret, with no swimming pool and everyone fully clothed," Artie said glumly.

While Mariel took a bath, Artie sat in the kitchen over toast, coffee, and the funnies. His lover reappeared shortly, still dripping, her robe hanging liberally open.

"Coming to bed soon?"

This question, even when posed first thing in the morning, was not a question to stump Artie Plask. He leapt up from his chair and pursued the pink, giggling dynamo of flesh and wit that was Mariel Fenton back into the bedroom.

As Artie crossed the threshold, gripping his hardness through his pajama bottoms, Mariel shed her robe and threw herself onto the prairie of their mattress, gathering around her the lone blanket that had not been thrown off when they arose. She lay on her side, cloaked in the plush fabric.

He knelt on the bed behind her. The edges of the blanket formed a curtain over Mariel's backside, and he lifted one corner to reveal a triangular section of ass – a brief line of ass crack surrounded by small samples of cheek on each side.

He gave his full attention to this derriere microcosm, stroking and fondling all that was visible as if it were the only flesh in the world ... a sentient, pleasure-loving thing in its own right that thrived on his stimulation. With Mariel's face – indeed the entire rest of Mariel – temporarily invisible, it was this compact portion of her bottom that Artie was making love to, kissing and caressing, driving wild.

Gradually he let his hands travel from the hills down toward her valley, teasing and exploring until he found her seam, the slick entrance into the whole ... the welcoming slot tucked snugly within the lowlands.

She lifted her head. "Mmm ... yes, Artie, take me from behind. I understand it's supposed to bring good luck in the morning."

He chuckled. "You just made that up, didn't you?"

"Mmm-hmm."

He gave her a place-holding finger-streak along her moistening lips before leaving the bed to undress and rubber up.

When he rejoined her, he found her even wetter than before. Her pussy flesh, swimming in its ripeness like breakfast melon, felt slippery-sweet as his shaft sank into it.

# Chapter 20

The Startled Egret – with no swimming pool and everyone fully clothed – was precisely where they happened to be a little later, when Mariel spotted Lionel Stimpson heading their way. She nudged Artie to alert him.

Lionel swaggered up to their table. "You're the writers I met on the train, aren't you." It was a statement, not a question, Stimpson being presumably too interested in his own continuing discourse to want the distraction of a reply. "You said you wrote a sports program, yes?" This one was actually a question.

Artie didn't know where the fellow had obtained such an idea, but he recognized the wisdom of Mariel's decision in letting him keep it. "That's right," she said. "I'm flattered that you remember."

"I have an astounding memory," Lionel explained. "It's quite magnificent."

Artie felt his eyebrows – his true eyebrows, this not being a disguise day – climbing up his forehead. In an attempt to change the subject, he nodded at the book tucked under the playwright's arm. "What are you reading?"

"It's a history of art," Lionel answered, in a tone suggesting he might personally be able to take credit for every masterpiece mentioned in its pages.

"Ah," said Mariel. "Well, I won't spoil the ending for you."

"Don't be absurd – I've read it before, of course," Stimpson snapped. "I'm rereading it as inspiration for my new play, which will be set in the world of art. There's so much ugliness there."

"At least there will be now," Artie said under his breath.

"Yes," Lionel continued, "I've decided radio is beneath me."

"I see," said Mariel agreeably. "*You* decided that, eh?"

"I was going to elevate the medium. But why waste my immense talent on so unworthy a vehicle?"

And with that, he nodded semipolitely and left them.

Mariel was scowling.

"Don't let him ruin your day," Artie cajoled. "Here – would you like my pickle?"

Her hand shot out reflexively toward his groin; so he directed her other hand to the kosher dill on his plate.

"There's something phony about that guy," Mariel mused juicily while she munched.

"From where I sit, there's *everything* phony about that guy. So what? I've only been here a short time, but I've gathered this town is not completely lacking in that personality type."

"That's just it. After knocking around Hollywood my entire adult life, I know my phonies. And though I can't put my finger on why, I think Lionel Stimpson is a *phony* phony."

She worked her way down the pickle. "I wonder who he is underneath ... and what he's up to."

The next day, Artie and Mariel arrived ahead of the others for the afternoon script session on *The Elyse Heffernan Show*, with the intention of running some new lines by Elyse to make sure they worked in her voice.

They found her alone by the pool in a tennis outfit, studying a script with a hand under her skirt. She smiled up at them as they came through the patio door – leaving her hand where it was.

"I guess I have my hand under my skirt," she said.

"Yes, we noticed," said Mariel collegially.

"You'll never guess who phoned me this morning," their hostess said after they'd sat down – Artie with slight difficulty. "Lionel Stimpson." Elyse made a sour-lemons face as she spoke the name, and her masturbation hand temporarily halted in sympathy.

"Interesting," said Artie.

"Very," said Mariel. "What did he want?"

"He wants to cast me in one of those dreadful plays of his. Can you believe it? Even leaving aside how terrible his writing is, I loathe Lionel Stimpson. I don't want to work with him ... I don't want to *speak* to him. I don't even want to *fuck* him."

"But he wants you."

Elyse nodded. "He explained that while no cast on earth could possibly do justice to his work, his next play will have the cast that's come closest to date. He said he'd just been on the phone with Lila Lowell, who had immediately accepted the part he'd offered her."

"You're kidding," said Artie.

Mariel stood up. "Let me get this straight, Elyse. Stimpson said he'd spoken personally to Lila on the telephone."

Elyse nodded again.

Mariel threw Artie a look of shrewd satisfaction.

"What is it?" he said.

"Don't you get it? He said he spoke to Lila *on the phone*. Lila Lowell wouldn't speak to her own mother on the phone, remember?"

"You mean he lied to me?" said Elyse.

"Undoubtedly. The only question is *why?*" said Mariel.

There was quiet for a moment, except for the honeyed soundtrack of Elyse's fingers in her cunt.

"You don't mind if I keep touching myself while we talk, do you? I always think better when I do."

"Go right ahead," said Mariel. "It's not bothering you *too* much, is it, Artie?"

"I never understood why Daddy wanted to work with Lionel in the first place. Really, that play he wrote for Daddy was unbelievably awful."

"Yes ... *unbelievably* awful," Mariel repeated slowly.

This time Artie was with her. "You mean *phony* awful?"

"Exactly," said Mariel. "Stimpson may be a very capable writer at that – a talented imitator of all that is lousy in lousy drama, whose only failing is that he went too far for it to be credible to an astute observer."

"Yes," said Artie, "I see."

"And, again, the only question is *why?*"

"Yeah ... why ... ," Artie repeated thoughtfully.

"Why," Elyse echoed quietly, holding the syllable in her mouth as her eyes grew large. "Wh – wh – oh god – wh – "

She closed her eyes and let the question drop uncompleted, as she squeezed her tennis-skirted-thighs around her hidden fingers and came.

Around lunchtime, Lubb interrupted the writers to call Elyse to the phone. She returned a few minutes later.

Someone from the network was wondering if she thought her sponsor – being based in Los Angeles, as they'd inferred – might like to participate in an upcoming event in front of their building, a publicity gig that Elyse herself had already agreed to.

"They thought you might want to bring some mannequins," she explained to Mariel. "They said something about raffling one of them off."

Mariel said she'd check with her uncle to see if he could drive down with a minyan of mannequins on Wednesday, the day of the event. "And we can ask Henry to get his hands on some used costumes for us."

"That raffle angle is funny, though," she added after a moment. "Who's going to want a mannequin as a door prize?"

"You'd be surprised," said Artie. "If someone back home had offered me Trixie, I certainly would have made room for her in my walk-up."

"Yes, but you're a special kind of pervert."

"Thank you," said Artie graciously.

# Chapter 21

Mariel, Elyse, and "Mr. Trixton" arrived early for the publicity affair downtown.

"Shall we cool our heels in the coffee shop?" suggested Mariel, while they scouted the block for a parking place. "Mert won't be here for at least another thirty minutes, I'm sure."

"I wonder if I might prefer the drugstore," said Elyse. "It has a soda fountain, you know, and soda fountains make my panties moist."

"Again I must point out that nearly everything makes your panties moist," said Mariel kindly. "Which is wonderful, of course ... but I don't see how you can go very far with it as a decision-making criterion."

Elyse shrugged, insofar as her driving posture permitted it. "It's worked pretty well thus far."

Once in the drugstore, Elyse posed with self-aware but un-self-conscious glamour on a stool.

"You want some ice cream?" the druggist asked her.

"No, thank you," said Elyse. "I've just come to swivel."

"And possibly vice versa," Artie quipped in an undertone.

"*I* will have some ice cream," said Mariel.

While they waited for the ice cream, Artie let himself be hypnotized by Elyse's swinging legs as she pivoted on her stool – presumably endowing it with her scent.

"Oh, look," said Mariel, just after she'd started on her sundae. "Here comes Crane from the network."

The amiable young executive made his way over and greeted Elyse and Mariel.

"Mr. Crane," said Mariel, "this is Mr. Trixton of Metropolitan Mannequins."

The men shook hands.

"And how are things in the writing room?" Crane inquired.

"It's not really a room, it's more of a swimming pool ... but things are going swell," said Mariel.

Crane nodded politely. "I'm glad I caught you all here," he said. "It seems there's a slight problem with our proceeding as planned this afternoon."

Artie didn't like the sound of that, and he wasn't surprised to see Mariel's eyes narrow in response to the executive's statement – though in his opinion the effect was undercut by the fact that she continued spooning ice cream into her mouth.

"A problem? What sort of problem?" Mariel inquired. And, before Crane could answer, she inquired further, "A problem for *whom?*" She smacked her lips briefly as she articulated the grammatically correct terminal *m*, seizing the dessert-savoring possibilities the phoneme presented.

Crane looked suitably sheepish. "For – er – the mannequins, actually. It's all my fault, I'm afraid – terrible handwriting, and my typist was off that day. So where I wrote *Metropolitan Mannequins* on the copy for the posters, the printer thought I'd written *Helicoptering Marquesses*. So that's what the posters say – they're all over town, you understand – and apparently the public is expecting some kind of daredevil act. I've only just found out."

"Helicoptering Marquesses?" Artie repeated incredulously.

"Yes. Fortunately, we have some circus types under contract, for fill-in programming – I've never understood why people are entertained by *listening* to acrobats they can't see, but they are – and I've been assured that they can become helicoptering marquesses for the purposes of today's event. But they're going to require a lot of space for their act, and I'm afraid that won't leave room for any mannequins. As it is, we're going to have a hell of a time making room for you and your cast," he said to Elyse. "And the terms of our permit from the city won't allow us to block off any more space out there in front of the building."

"I can't believe you would stand there and tell us we can't bring our mannequins to your party," said Mariel. "For Pete's sake, you're going to break Artie Plask's heart." She jerked her thumb in Artie's direction.

Crane looked confused. "Why did you call him 'Artie Plask'? I thought this was Trixton."

"Huh?" said Mariel. "Oh … it's … it's a term of endearment." She gave Artie a sisterly stroke on the bicep. "And please don't change the subject."

But there was, according to Crane, nothing to be done. And thus it was a grumbling Mariel and Artie who soon stood on the sidewalk awaiting Mert.

He pulled up a short time later with an assortment of nude, especially lovely mannequins lolling in the open back of his truck – and one item that was, Artie decided, either an attempt at a cubist mannequin or a stray floor lamp. Their busy schedule had meant he and Mariel had yet to see Mert's handiwork; and so despite the cloud that had passed over the occasion due to Crane's blunder, this was a moment to be savored with pride.

"They're gorgeous," Artie proclaimed.

"So vivacious looking, Mert!" Mariel added.

Then she broke the news that he and the ladies had driven all this way for nothing.

"Well, that's not exactly true," Mert said slowly. He was not his usual jovial self, and it was obvious to Artie that something more than a fouled-up publicity opportunity was on the uncle's mind.

"What do you mean?" asked Mariel.

"I mean I would've had to drive down here to round up the other mannequins anyway."

"What?"

"I guess it's good that I can tell you in person," said Mert. "But not here. After this network thing you're doing is over, we'll drive back to your place and have a talk, okay?"

They made their way into the apartment. Mariel got some Scotch into their hands, and they all settled themselves in the living room.

"I'm afraid we've been getting complaints," said Mert.

"Complaints?" said Mariel. "What kind of complaints?"

"It has to do with how the mannequins smell."

"How the mannequins *smell?*" said Mariel.

"But mannequins don't have any noticeable smell," Artie protested. "Do they?" He looked from Mert to Mariel and back.

"I guess they're not supposed to," Mert acknowledged.

"What, do *your* mannequins smell like real women?" Mariel asked.

"Oh, no. If they did, I'd probably have kept them all for myself."

"Well, what, then?" said Artie.

"Chewing gum," Mert answered seriously.

"Huh?"

"They smell sort of like gum – unflavored gum. Lots of it. It's the latex. See, when we first got into this, I did a little research on the state of mannequin making, like you asked me to. I found out that people have been talking about trying plaster, as a way to improve on the ol' wood-and-wax technique that had your friend cursing on the floor of his shop. But me, I thought I'd try rubber instead. Because, like I said before, a mannequin's really nothing but a big doll.

I made thousands of rubber dolls, in my day – so why not rubber mannequins, right?"

"Seems logical," said Artie.

"But, see, kids don't mind if their dolls smell like gum."

"And clothing-store proprietors, I suppose, do," said Mariel.

"Correct," Mert sighed. "If only because their customers do."

"I didn't notice any odor when I ogled the ones in the back of your truck today."

"But remember, Artie, that was outdoors."

"Precisely," said Mert. "Now, you get a few of these dolls inside the four walls of a boutique, and it's another story. If our clients are to be believed, ladies are walking around sniffing the air and asking each other snootily, 'Maxine, darling, you're not chewing gum, are you?' The stores feel this is an undesirable distraction from shopping."

"Ah," said Mariel.

"Nor could I interest them in replacing these dolls with anything else that Met Mannequins might come up with. Basically, that emblem on the heinie has become a guaranteed no-sale."

"Ah," said Mariel.

Artie couldn't recall the last evening he'd spent without Mariel. Nor could he recall the last time in his life there'd *been* anyone he'd spent evening after evening with.

He'd left Mariel and Mert at her place, discussing the logistics of dissolving the Metropolitan Mannequin Company. Feeling he had nothing to contribute in that area, Artie had suggested he go on ahead to his own apartment, where some long-neglected cleaning tasks awaited him. Mariel would join him there at bedtime, leaving Mert to sleep over in her bedroom at home.

Alone in his apartment now, he marveled at how life with Mariel and the rest of her circle was proving to be precisely what he'd asked for in jest: a series of smaller orgies; a quip come true. He smirked at the thought. In spite of the bad news that Mert had delivered, Artie was conscious of how happy he was.

He rolled up his sleeves to wash some dishes and, as an afterthought, switched on the radio.

His face lit up when he realized he'd tuned in during a block of Spanish-language programming. Exercising his Spanish listening comprehension seemed an ideal way to add some interest to household chores. It was even a comedy show that was airing at the moment.

But the eager smile of the language student was soon replaced by the horrified, incredulous stare of the plagiarism victim.

His internal phrase book provided Artie with a service-able simultaneous translation:

*"Miss Evans, this is your attorney, Mr. Pockington."*

*"Oh, hello, Pockets!"*

*"Now, Miss Evans, I have a great deal of unfinished business on my desk."*

*"Well, I – just a minute. There's someone at the door. Come innnnnnn!"*

*"G'morning, Miss Evans."*

*"Hello, Wainscot. I'll be with you in a minute. My friend Pockets is on the phone, and I need to help him with his unfinished business."*

Artie's mouth gaped open. Though the voices – and the altered but still-anglophonic character names – were unfamiliar, nothing else was.

Someone had stolen the first installment of *The Elyse Heffernan Show*, and sold a translated version.

# Chapter 22

As soon as Mariel arrived, Artie told her what had come over the dial.

She was blindsided by the news – a novelty in itself, Artie had to assume.

"Does Elyse know? Mickey?"

He shook his head. "Not unless they discovered it independently. I wanted to talk to you about it first. It crossed my mind that you might have – well, that maybe you were somehow behind it ... that expanding into the Spanish-language market without telling anyone might be part of some brilliant, tricky scheme of yours that even I didn't know about."

Her eyes softened. "Oh, Artie. I would never keep one of my brilliant, tricky schemes from you. We're sort of ... partners, right?" She took his hand.

"Right." He squeezed her palm.

Mariel got back to business – and outrage. "So what-thepardonmyFrenchfuck?" she muttered indignantly.

Artie was nonplussed as well. Petty pilfering was a common annoyance in the entertainment business, but this large-scale act of larceny was another matter.

A quick pair of phone calls confirmed that neither Elyse nor Mickey knew. Elyse seemed to take the news in stride; whereas when Artie unveiled the crime for Mickey, the nasal buzz of expletives that came through the phone resembled an irate oboe.

Mariel was pacing as she thought things out. "I happen to know a little about the way these Spanish-language broadcasts work. They're under the control of brokers, who subcontract the time from the stations and provide their own content. It's a smart arrangement – it serves a lot of listeners that the stations themselves won't bother with."

"Right," said Artie.

"Now, these brokers are usually Spanish-speaking entertainment providers themselves, creating their own programs. But ..."

"Yes?"

"Suppose there's a broker out there who's merely an entrepreneur. Someone who doesn't even speak Spanish, but who somehow got into this business. He would secure the air time, hire the entertainment, and maybe acquire some material for them."

"And ...?"

"And if someone he trusted approached him with a Spanish-language comedy script, *he wouldn't know what was in it.*"

"So he wouldn't realize it was the same program he'd heard Elyse do a couple of weeks earlier."

"Exactly. He'd just buy the script from his trusted source, figuring it was good stuff, and pass it on to his performers."

"And though *they* might recognize it as our show, they wouldn't question its provenance. For all they know, it was legally licensed. They would just go on the air and do it."

"Right."

"Wow," said Artie.

"All of which raises the question: who is the 'trusted source'?"

"Yes," said Artie. "Someone unprincipled, of course."

"Someone with a facility for writing – in at least two languages."

"Someone with access to our scripts, probably ... unless he took it down in shorthand when it aired, which would be – oh, no! You don't think it's one of our writing team, do you?"

"No, Artie, on the contrary, I think it's someone who felt he'd been *wronged* by our writing team, and who saw an opportunity to make a quick buck at our expense."

Mariel hadn't been to the Argyle Avenue Playhouse in years. They produced few comedies, and her appetite for serious drama was limited. The last time she'd been here, she'd been in the company of a Dada composer she was sleeping with, who wanted to see his sister carry a bucket across the stage in a rustic allegory. Not a memorable role for the poor young woman, who had not yet graduated to "ingénue"; but to her credit she had not spilled a drop of the imaginary water, and Mariel had duly congratulated her.

She spotted Lionel, as advertised, in the back row, but she didn't let her gaze linger on him, lest he notice her. She'd decided to steer clear of him prior to curtain time, convinced that their conversation would go more smoothly after she'd taken in his play – and confirmed that he was capable of good work when not deliberately producing bad. Yes, though comedy was her bailiwick, Mariel had a hunch that *This Petty Pace*, despite the nuisance of its obligatory Shakespearean-coattails title, would prove to be a fine little drama.

She was correct. The spare, compelling story unfolded over a lean ninety minutes, holding her spellbound with its deceptively simple language, language so seamlessly graceful Mariel had the illusion of reading the characters' minds – as if the author were so adroit that speech was unnecessary.

It was, in short, the opposite of the bloated, garish, ungainly prose that Lionel Stimpson had written for Sid Heffy.

Stimpson was not difficult to locate in the lobby afterward. And yet, had Mariel not been certain she recognized his physical features – his long neck, his impenetrable gray eyes, and his slight underbite – she would have doubted that this was he. For his manner, even observed from a distance, was entirely different from what she'd had ample opportunity to experience on previous occasions. He seemed humbly hungry for praise, and visibly grateful for the few compliments that the jaded theatergoers deigned to supply. And in this mode he was, Mariel realized with a bit of a shock, sexually attractive to her. Quite.

"That was an outstanding play," she said after creeping up on him from one side, her small stature working in her favor by keeping her out of his sight line.

"Thank you," he answered quickly and heartily, turning to seek out the source of the praise. His face froze when he recognized her. "Oh, hello," he said tentatively. "We spoke at the Egret, didn't we?"

"Yes," said Mariel. "And on the train."

"Yesssss ... the train," Stimpson allowed. "Forgive me, though – do I know your name?"

"I've never *told* you my name, if that's what you mean. But I think you know it nonetheless, Lionel. I think you've known it all along."

"What do you mean?"

"You write so beautifully."

"Thank you."

"It's not a compliment this time, Lionel. It's an accusation. Shall we have a drink next door?"

# Chapter 23

Lionel matched her Scotch with a whiskey order of his own. As Mariel had suspected, the never-drinking-except-on-vacation rule had just been part of the put-on, a colorful detail that Stimpson had added to what she now dubbed the "Arrogant Stimpson" mystique.

"I'm sorry I pulled your leg, Mariel," he said earnestly.

"Well, that's all right," she replied. "After all, I don't personally own any body part that's better suited to pulling. And, hell, it was entertaining. Oh, how we snickered at your vanity and your preposterous claptrap."

Lionel winced. "I hope you'll let me explain."

"That's why we're here."

"When Aunt Lentilla – "

"*Aunt* Lentilla?

He nodded. "Yes, dear Aunt Lentilla. She means well, but I'm afraid she's one of those people who's burdened with a perennially misdirected altruism. You know, the type who goes through life offering dog biscuits to cats. And when she asked – or rather *insisted* – I take the Sid Heffy gig, I was horrified."

"Not a fan of Sid's work, eh?"

Lionel set his drink down. "Oh, no, Mariel – on the contrary. I consider Heffy our greatest comedian," he said, with unmistakable sincerity.

The admission took Mariel by surprise, and she set her drink down as well.

"I've thought so since I was the merest lad," Lionel added, slipping back into the idiom of Arrogant Stimpson. Mariel, catching this lapse, wagged a finger at him.

"Sorry – since I was a boy. Sure, I write dramas now, but comedy was my first love. So when I learned that Aunt Lentilla wanted a playwright to assist Heffy in denaturing radio's finest comedy show into serious drama – and that she expected me to do the dirty work – I was, as I say, horrified."

"But you took the job."

"Yes, I took the job. For two reasons: First, I'm not generally in a position to refuse when my aunt assigns a job to me. You see, I don't quite make a living writing plays, and she's the one who ..."

"I get the picture." In truth, she'd already guessed that part of it. "What was the other reason?"

"The other reason was that somewhere in the process of bemoaning the situation, I had an important insight – you might even call it a stroke of brilliance."

"You're sounding like your self-infatuated persona again."

Lionel shook his head. "No, my self-infatuated persona would have said stroke of *genius*. Anyway, this is what occurred to me: as the playwright saddled with the task of creating *The Sidney Heffy Dramatic Culture Hour*, I would automatically become the person in the best position to *sabotage it*."

He smiled at her, raising his glass to his lips. She admired the sensitivity in his mouth, and the handsome line of his jaw. Nor did she neglect to appreciate the rare privilege of being face to face with someone whose capacity for chutzpah, in the interest of some worthwhile goal, possibly exceeded even her own.

"Once I'd realized I had not only the opportunity but, as I saw it, an obligation to Western civilization to do what I could to derail the nauseating scheme, I accepted the job with enthusiasm and proceeded with my mission."

"No disputing that it was noble of you," said Mariel sincerely. "But – not to detract from your glory – don't you think Heffy was fully capable of derailing the program on his own? He stinks at drama."

"Yes – and indeed I expected he would. But since no one had yet heard him doing drama, I couldn't be sure at the time. In any event, I didn't want to count on his ineptness alone guaranteeing the new format's failure. I'm a writer, and ultimately I trusted writing to do the job. You can understand that, I'm sure."

"Yeah, I guess I can. So you got busy writing Sid the lousiest material you could."

"Once I got going, I found I enjoyed it. Letting myself run wild with inadvisable literary techniques, and playing the part of the insufferable self-styled genius. Technically I didn't need to do *that*, of course; but, well, I used to do a little acting, and I suppose I've missed it."

"You certainly made up for lost acting time as far as the shtick was concerned."

He looked pleased but sheepish. "The only time I didn't like it was when Elyse was around. My jerk act made her hate me, naturally, and I would have preferred very much for Elyse in particular to like me. If you know what I mean."

"All of Hollywood knows what you mean."

She looked at Lionel Stimpson – humble, approachable, daringly resourceful Lionel Stimpson – and pictured his sensitive face between Elyse's legs, his delicate fingers sparking against Elyse's nipples. The whiskey was warming Mariel's blood, and much of the heat seemed to center in her panties. Lionel was making her wet.

She watched his face and his body language as he continued.

"The irony was that although she didn't know it, Elyse and I were allies. While she challenged her father by launching her comedy show, I was busy destroying his dramatic program. It was the combination of our efforts –

*your* efforts and my own – that brought such a speedy end to *The Sidney Heffy Dramatic Culture Hour*."

"Nice touch, making it a full hour."

He grinned. "Yes. But I can't take credit for that one – it was Heffy's idea. Can you imagine?"

"We didn't have to imagine. We heard it."

They both laughed. Suddenly Mariel stopped short, having realized something. "Oh! Then ... on the train ... you *intentionally* tipped us off that Sid planned to double-cross us by reverting to drama after pretending to give in."

"You have no idea how many meals I ate at the Egret that week, waiting in vain for you to show up. And then I tripped over you in a railroad car instead."

"And then, ignorant of your good deed, we turned around and got you fired."

"That you did. But of course that wasn't the real me, and I *wanted* to be fired. It meant I'd succeeded in my self-appointed task, and it would be up to you to block Heffy's next dramatic gambit – which, having heard the recent programs, I can say you've managed ingeniously."

"Thank you, Lionel," Mariel said with warmth. She liked this sexy man very much.

Then she remembered the immediate issue that had brought her here.

"But wait a minute – since you *wanted* to get fired, why in the world did you steal a script from *The Elyse Heffernan Show* and sell it to Spanish radio? We thought you'd done it out of spite. Did Aunt Lentilla's allowance run short on you?"

Lionel broke into uncontrollable laughter, attracting the attention of nearby patrons. "You – ahahaha – you thought *I* did that? Oh, Mariel, you wrong me ..." Another round of laughter consumed him.

"What? But then who – "

Lionel took a sip of whiskey to settle himself down.

"It was Lubb, naturally. He's been pirating Heffy's scripts for a couple of years, and now he's simply added Elyse to his portfolio."

"*What?*"

"It's the truth. As I understand it, Lubb has a confederate – a crooked Berlitz teacher – who does the translations, and they split the profits. Aunt Lentilla got wind of the racket a long time ago, but she was always afraid to break the news to Sid. I understand he and Lubb go all the way back to Heffy's days as a vaudeville star."

"And nobody else with a stake in the show ever tuned in to Spanish radio?"

Lionel shrugged. "Did *you?*"

Mariel took a moment to absorb everything. "So meanwhile, the broker who's buying the scripts assumes that since he's buying them from Heffy's butler, Sid has authorized their sale."

Lionel burst into laughter again. "Almost – but not quite."

"What do you mean?"

He took another drink. "You see, the non-Spanish-speaking Spanish-radio broker is also a little nearsighted, I guess ... and when Lubb visits him to deliver the goods, he pretends that he *is* Sid Heffy. Payable in cash."

"Wow," said Mariel.

"And I accept your apology for thinking I was a script thief."

"I'm sorry, Lionel. You're not a thief."

He nodded forgivingly.

"You're just a liar."

"A liar? What do you mean? To whom did I lie?"

"To Elyse."

"Elyse? About what?"

"About Lila Lowell taking a part in your next play."

"Oh. That. Yes. Er ... how do you know it isn't true?"

"The fact that you expressly said she spoke to you on the phone. Those of us who are close to Lila know that she has an unquenchable aversion to the telephone. You blundered by making your lie too specific," she summed up, drawing on every detective skit she'd ever penned for the Heffy show.

He looked contrite. "I just wanted to make it more attractive to Elyse. I wanted a chance to work with her, to start over on good terms and without any playacting – so to speak. The offer was on the level. I have a grand role for her –"

"Lionel ..."

"Sorry. I have an *excellent part* in my play – my play about the art world – that I know she'd be lovely with. I was going to tell her a little later that Lila had backed out."

Mariel took a sip of Scotch, and then held the glass just under her lips. "Well, Lionel, you were at the head of the class when it came to portraying Hollywood's most self-infatuated young prince of the playhouses. But when it comes to boudoir time with Elyse Heffernan, you'll have to get in line with the rest of us. Granted, it's a line that moves briskly."

"To be honest, I'm more interested now in casting her than bedding her. The woman is brilliant on that program you've created. Not that I'd say no to some carnal dalliance."

Mariel sighed wearily. "Lionel ..."

"Sorry. I should have said *fucking*, of course."

She gulped some more Scotch. "Just think, if I weren't sitting here to rectify your lapses into pretentious vocabulary, you'd soon be making an ass of yourself all over town."

"Nonsense. There are some parts of town my business never takes me. Still, I'm delighted that you're sitting there."

"So am I." She left the thought dangling in the air a moment, waiting to see if he would grab it. When it dropped ungrasped, she took it up awkwardly and tossed it into the air again, so that she could catch it in a sounder grip. "You're nice to talk to, when you're really yourself."

"Thank you."

"I imagine you're nice to do other things to as well."

His cool gray eyes widened slightly. "Are you ...?"

"You know, Lionel, Artie and I aren't possessive about each other." She hoped no further clarifications would be necessary; at this point she was so aroused she was sure there was a damp spot on her seat.

She watched him studying her for several seconds.

"Mariel, allow me to remark that you'd be a delectable person to have naked straddling one's lap," he finally said. "Sorry," he added. "Was *delectable* too pretentious an adjective?"

"It was perfect," said Mariel. She leaned across the table and kissed him wetly.

# Chapter 24

"So," said Lionel, as they stepped out into the mild night air, "shall we go upstairs?"

Mariel looked around. "You live nearby?"

He shook his head. "Upstairs at the playhouse. There's a room they keep ready for when we occasionally have a visiting actor. Which we non-visiting people make sure the company gets its money's worth out of the rest of the time."

"I love show people," said Mariel.

"As long as the key's on its hook in the box office, the room is all ours."

The key was indeed on its hook in the now-empty building, and Lionel led her up a back stairway to a carpeted corridor. They passed an office, a prop room, and a wardrobe repository on their way to the visiting players' apartment.

"Now, what was that about someone straddling someone's lap?" Mariel inquired once they'd let themselves in.

She felt her libido sizzling under her skirt as she backed him toward the bed, enjoying the overwhelming sensation of not being able to keep her hands off Lionel a minute longer – and not needing to. She heard herself actually growl as she pushed him onto the mattress and climbed aboard his lap, pawing at his shirt buttons.

He responded in kind while they kissed, and in short order he was bare-chested and she bra-intimate. Then, while she stroked the fine fur that made a tentative path from his navel halfway to his nipples, Lionel unhitched the bra and let it fall onto his crotch. Her breasts became pleasure-warmed rolls in his hands; she wiggled in half-naked heat, her clit twitching in her panties.

Lionel's cock, Mariel observed, was as elegantly formed as his play – though it did not, she noted cheerfully, replicate its brevity. She clutched it greedily, smoothing down the trouser fabric around the open fly; all she wanted at this moment, with every pussy-juice-saturated cell in her body, was to lower herself slowly – no, *quickly* – onto this fat stick of maleness and sit in the driver's seat until she was satisfied.

Like Artie, Lionel believed in being prepared ... and no sooner was that matter attended to, and Mariel's skirt and panties discarded, than she did exactly what she'd planned to do.

"Oh, fuuuuuuuuuuuuuuuuck," she crooned, her eyes three-quarters closed, as she engulfed him. Lionel groaned his lust back at her.

Soon she felt her ass gyrating in a frenzy upon his thighs, while her knees dug into the mattress and her cunt played piston on him at a crazy pace. Her mound humped his skinny abdomen, to send jolts to her clit.

Oh, yes, her body was fully engaged.

Her head spun with hedonistic affirmations while she fucked him and fucked him. How her pussy craved smart, beautiful men! How she loved their thick, pulsing cocks up her cunt, and their tender faces melting into ecstasy before her eyes. Like Artie. Like Lionel. Like *this*, *this*, *this*. The *this*es bounced in her head like hot marbles.

She was ready to come before he was – so ready, Mariel realized, that she couldn't hold back, couldn't possibly hold back ... and the pleasure that overtook her was so explosive she let out an honest-to-goodness scream that she knew was probably louder than many a stage scream delivered over the floorboards downstairs.

Now sated, she rolled over so that Lionel could pump her from above. She studied his preorgasmic face – so intent, so impassioned.

She felt the tickle of a wayward aftershock in her cunt when he came with a surprisingly deep roar. She churned her hips under his orgasm, wallowing in the unplanned horny deliciousness of it all.

"Do you mean to say that Stimpson was doing to the previous Heffy radio drama what we're in the process of doing to the current one?"

Artie had relished the details that Mariel had supplied of her ins and outs under the covers with Lionel the previous night, but he wasn't sure he understood all the ins and outs of the revelations that had preceded their romp.

"Not exactly. Lionel was deliberately writing laughably bad drama, with the goal of ruining any slight chance the program might have had for success. Whereas we, as you know, are writing good drama, then poking holes in it so as to turn it into laughably good comedy (while still keeping Sid convinced it's drama), with the goal of making the show succeed on our terms, and those of his public, while he thinks it's succeeding on his."

When Mariel spoke in such convoluted yet eloquent expository paragraphs, Artie half expected her to conclude with a "Yours, sincerely" or an "I will await your kind reply by return post." Her gift for expression was one of the reasons he loved this woman – and the "carpe diem" spirit that prompted her to do things like fuck another man's head off on the spur of the moment was another.

Musing on their professional state of affairs, he looked out the window at the deceptive placidity of the palm trees, the flowers, and the rain-cloud-free sky.

"Are things always this turbulent in Hollywood radio circles? Do we always spend this much time and energy shaking things up and swinging at curve balls? Staging diversions and chasing our tails?"

Mariel considered this. "No. It's just been an unusually busy spring. Why? Do you miss the peace and quiet of New York?"

"Not as long as you're out here."

She took his hand, and they looked out toward the mountains together.

"I think we could both do with a rest. Let's plan on a vacation soon."

"Beautiful," said Artie.

She put her hand in his rear trouser pocket. "It'll be a chance to unwind and" – she squeezed his ass – "*indulge*."

"Mmm."

"Just you and me," said Mariel.

"Mmm."

"And maybe Elyse. Mickey ... Lila and Nanette ..."

"Beautiful," said Artie again.

They turned back to the room. Mariel took a deep breath.

"So today: *Elyse Heffernan Show*; pre-show rehearsal at three."

"Check. Then the Heffy show tomorrow, of course ..."

"Preceded by Henry and Midge's wedding."

"Check."

Then Mariel mentioned the item neither of them wanted to confront. "Alas, we also have the unpleasant job of telling Elyse that tonight's show will be her last, now that the trademark Met Mannequin buttock has gone bust."

"Check ... and mate," said Artie sadly.

But Elyse proved surprisingly cheerful when they broke the news over lunch at the Egret.

"Well, maybe it's for the best. I'm going to be awfully busy rehearsing for Lionel's play now."

And she explained how Stimpson had shown up at the Heffy mansion first thing in the morning. "As soon as I saw him, I could tell that something was different – *he* was different."

Lionel had told her everything he'd told Mariel, omitting, Artie inferred, only the revelation that the family butler was pirating scripts on the side – a situation that the playwright, in the shadow of his aunt's inaction on the matter, looked upon as an applecart it was not his place to upset. Nor, Mariel and Artie had agreed, was it theirs. The long-standing Heffy-Lubb symbiosis seemed too sacred a formula to disrupt.

"His writing is so different, too!" Elyse bubbled on. "His *real* writing, I mean. Nothing like that dreck he created for Daddy. Of course, now I understand he did that deliberately." She giggled at the thought. "He showed me his new script. It's tremendous – and it's even about modern art." Out of everything under the sun, this was the thing Elyse was most interested in.

Apart from sex, swimming, and the company of humorists, naturally.

# Chapter 25

Artie couldn't imagine why the studio had permitted Henry and Midge to get married on the set of Lila's latest picture. And yet here they all were on Lila's soundstage, which for several weeks had been dressed for a wedding scene in her movie – a cinematic showpiece of a ceremony, in a designer's rather fanciful conception of a function room in a suburban town hall.

According to Mariel, the real-life bride and groom had left the timing of *their* ceremony open, waiting for this set to go up in the course of the shooting schedule. They had been very relaxed about keeping their wedding date up in the air, and nervous only about the possibility that the film's wedding scene might get cut from the script.

"Henry always wanted a real-fake-real Hollywood wedding," Mariel had recounted to Artie and Elyse on the drive over. "He's such a sentimentalist."

"How in the world did they get the front office to agree to this?" Artie asked her now, as they made their way to their seats.

"The front office thinks it's part of the movie. Look over there, for instance." She nodded toward a camera operator. "Of course, no director would really stage, light, or film a scene in quite this way. But what the front office knows about the technical side of moviemaking could be written in toto on one half of a torn-up casting agent's card – with an empty fountain pen."

"But what about the director? Surely, he would never tolerate this."

"No, he wouldn't. So it's a good thing Lila is treating him to a weekend in Palm Springs, isn't it?"

They took their seats and Artie looked around, spotting Lila and Nanette and a few other familiar faces – along with a generous number of motion-picture-business strangers, and two small clusters of what were presumably the wedding stars' respective family members, judging from their impeccable but subdued clothing and their open-mouthed, rib-elbowing, finger-pointing fascination with the lights and cameras.

The ceremony was stylish but uneventful, except for one awkward juncture when a ceremonial uncle, having just read a romantic poem, absentmindedly attempted to leave the set with something that he thought was his hat – something that was, in actuality, a set-piece hat that had been fastened securely to the hat rack with carpenters'-union-grade staples.

"Maybe they can use some of this in the movie after all," Mariel quietly commented as the uncle wrestled with the hat rack.

Once the vows had been exchanged, the soundstage became a sea of champagne, greetings, and congratulations. Mariel, who seemed to know everyone, introduced Artie left and right.

This phase of their afternoon lasted about ninety minutes, at which point Midge appeared at Mariel's elbow.

"Hello, sweetie. Private reception in Henry's building in fifteen minutes, okay?" She looked from Mariel to Artie, to make it clear that both were invited.

En route to the private reception, Artie appreciated more than ever the fact that Mariel knew her way around the lot. Gliding along in a pleasant champagne haze, his chances of finding Henry's building without her guidance would have been nil, rather than the usual slim. Even Mariel seemed to have to concentrate very intensely, in her tipsy state.

When they arrived in Henry's makeup room, they found the intimate party already in progress. Henry, Midge, Lila, Nanette, Elyse, and Mickey sat comfortably on a large rug in the middle of the floor – all of them naked. The newlyweds were holding hands, and Elyse was in Mickey's lap, but the sexuality in the room was fairly subdued, all things considered. It felt more like a gathering than an orgy.

Midge was hefting a bottle and addressing Lila: "Here, darling, pass me the left one, too. We're running a special." Until now, Artie had never actually seen someone pour champagne into footwear. He wondered if Henry kept a special supply of slippers for this purpose – perhaps in a crystal cabinet outfitted with shoe trees.

"Join the party," said their host with gusto when he noticed the new arrivals. "We thought it would be nice to have a little private time with our dear friends."

"Shall we?" said Mariel to Artie, gesturing toward the piles of clothing that covered one of Henry's work tables – which seemed to have been expressly cleared so as to accommodate the apparel of disrobing guests. The tableau of casually removed gowns, suits, and underwear – in a context where hangers, many of them empty, lined the walls – was something that Artie found erotic, like eating chocolate mousse off a lover's fingers instead of with a dessert spoon.

Once they'd undressed, Mariel took Artie's hand and they claimed a vacant section of the rug. Mariel lay on her tummy, and Artie sat cross-legged at her side, with one eye on her round, cheerful buttocks.

"This is beautiful, Henry," said Mariel.

Henry glowed with appreciation.

"Look at all our sweet, beautiful friends," Mariel gushed on. "Our sweet, beautiful, naked friends. Aren't we lucky, Artie?" Artie noticed that as she spoke, her right ass cheek vibrated slightly with the energy of her oration. He placed a hand there, to feel the lively tremors.

Henry cleared his throat. "Lila has an announcement to make."

"Yes," said Nanette, breaking into the expectant hush. "Lila wants you all to know that we'll be moving to New York in a couple of months. She's going to be on Broadway next season!"

Everyone applauded.

"Are you and Midge staying here?" Mickey asked Henry.

"Don't be absurd!" Lila had fielded that one herself, in a penetrating whisper.

"Don't be absurd," Henry echoed, laughing. "Naturally, we're going as well. Why, Lila wouldn't even make an appearance at my wedding today without having me do her makeup first. And I'll have you know she interrupted the wedding party at a *very* inconvenient time." He laughed generously again.

"Oh, come now, darling," said Midge, tickling him under his chin. "I think you liked watching me sit there patiently with my bare boobies while you took care of the boss." She turned to the others and winked. "It's ironic – he's always *smearing* whatever makeup *I* have on."

Henry helped himself to what his wife had described as a bare booby, and general conversation resumed – mostly on the topic of how much the Broadway-bound quartet would be missed.

Suddenly Elyse stood up. "What's that?"

She took down a hanger. It held the top half of what looked to Artie like a Hollywood conception of a "frontier schoolmarm" outfit.

As Elyse slipped on the blouse, string tie, and faux-buckskin jacket, Mickey reached helpfully for the long skirt that completed the costume.

"No, thank you, Mickey Licky, that won't be necessary."

And so what stood before them moments later was schoolmarm from the waist up, and just Elyse from the waist down.

"What a wonderful idea!" Mariel shouted, scrambling to her feet. "You don't mind if we play dress-up, do you, Henry?"

"Or, as the case may be, dress-partially-up," said Artie, treating himself to another long look at bare-bushed, buck-naked-assed, buckskin-wearing Elyse.

With Henry's consent, a mirthful race began for the costumes.

Artie, having had his fill of dressing himself up thanks to countless days spent under russet eyebrows, decided this would be a good time to avail himself of the washroom. He threw on his shirt, trousers, and socks and told the gang he'd be right back.

As he strolled down the corridor, he heard someone walking behind him. He turned and saw that it was Lila, who had donned a robe and was probably on an errand similar to his own. He paused to let her catch up with him.

"Artie-Artie," said Lila, evidently quite lightheaded – and considerably less inhibited than usual – after several slipperfuls of champagne. She took him by the arm. "I'm going to miss your Mariel."

"Yes," he said sympathetically. "I can imagine."

"I called her 'your' Mariel, but of course I knew her long before you did," Lila continued in a rambling alto.

It was interesting to Artie to see how the sloshingly discursive tipsy Lila differed from both the timid sober private Lila and the poised, magnetic cinematic Lila.

"But you and she ... great team. She – "

Suddenly, they became aware of an exuberant commotion from the direction of Henry's workroom. Their friends, in various cinematic getups that Artie couldn't im-mediately parse – and various degrees of inebriation that he could – were spilling out into the hall in a festive clump.

"Come 'ere," said Lila. "More private." And she pulled him through the door to her left – the ladies' room.

Once inside, he glanced around to make sure they were alone. Though sneaking into the ladies' room with a gorgeous movie star was inherently thrilling to Artie – and the situation furthermore suggested a scenario that was, thanks to Mariel, only too vividly accessible to his imagination – he was quite sure that this particular woman had not brought him here so that he could watch her pee. No, she simply wanted to continue their chat.

"Mariel." Lila said. "She loves you a bunch. But, of course, you know."

"I do. And the feeling, of course, is mutual."

"But I wanted to say it, 'cause I know it too. Firsthand."

He was touched. "Mariel was telling you how crazy she is about me, huh?"

Lila shook her head. "No – not in words, anyway. But I've seen the way she looks at you when your back is turned. So ..." The champagne-tickled movie star paused, gazing at him benevolently. "So ... I just wanted to bring you in here and say that."

"Thank you." He gave her shoulder a grateful squeeze, knowing tonight might be the only time she would welcome such a gesture.

"I'm going to miss her," Lila said again, with a misty-eyed smile.

"I can well imagine," Artie said again.

"And now, Artie-Artie, we must part company, you and I."

"Of course."

He left her to her privacy, and made his way across the corridor.

When he came out of the men's washroom, he calculated that the revelers had either returned to Henry's room or – more likely, given the air of effervescent entropy he'd observed – progressed around a corner to revel in additional portions of the building.

He was overjoyed when, a moment later, Mariel appeared around one such corner – having either turned around or completed a lap.

She moved toward him in a tipsy canter, wearing lilac panties and an unbuttoned paisley vest (or, assuming a screenplay set in London, *waistcoat*). Instead of her cloche, she was crowned with the floppier variety of chef's hat. She looked ridiculous, adorable, and irresistibly desirable, all at once.

Ironically, when they collided in a giggling embrace, it was she who commented on *his* appearance. Artie hadn't bothered to dress carefully when leaving Henry's premises, and he'd noticed in the washroom mirror that he had one cuff up and one down, and a collar that was indulging in a similar asymmetry. In addition, his hair had gone a little wild in the course of his jaunts into and out of the ladies' lounge.

"You look like the Pickwick Papers." Mariel said.

He tried to visualize the Dickens protagonist. "I look like Mr. Pickwick?"

"No, not *Mister* Pickwick," Mariel giggled. "The *papers*. You're all disheveled."

She French-kissed him hard, and he fondled her bottom through the silk.

Before he'd even had a chance to raise the question of what they'd do next – or rather *where* – she was taking his cock out of his trousers, complimenting him in passing on the absence of undershorts.

He reached for her lilac gusset. As they necked and she groped him, he stroked her softly, his fingers waiting alertly for the wetness to arrive. It didn't take long.

"Oh, yes," Mariel said with hot breath on his earlobe. "Let's do it right here."

"Look!" She broke the embrace and pointed to a rolled carpet fragment that had been left, for some reason, leaning against the wall a few yards down the hall. They raced toward it – Artie with his dick hanging out – and quickly had it in service beneath them like a picnicking couple's fuck blanket. They knelt together on the carpet while Artie got his condom into place.

Mariel bowed her head toward his rubber-clad tool and sniffed. "Maxine, darling, you're not chewing gum, are you?"

He burst out laughing at her antics, grabbing her by the middle. He tickled, then tackled, and soon was pressing his weight down on her, caressing her through her panties until her hips were bucking.

He slid the silk down her thighs and kissed her pussy; he licked the lips slowly, then dipped his tongue inside. He worked it around, then withdrew to give her clit some dainty swipes.

Her knees were stretching the panties. Artie took them the rest of the way off so his lover would be free to spread herself and receive all the pleasure she could take.

He ate her till she screamed, her pussy unabashedly honeying his face. Then he ate her some more.

She was still coming when he thrust his cock inside her – it seemed she never stopped coming in the short time it took him to dissolve into a delirious climax.

"Oh, Artie," Mariel said, in the voice of a woman recently fucked.

"Oh, Artie!" she said again – in the voice of a woman who has just realized she and her boyfriend are in danger of being late for a professional obligation. "We need to head back to Hollywood pronto, or we'll never be on time for Sid's show!"

They scrambled back to Henry's workroom, leaving the carpet remnant spread out for the next picnicking couple that might come along.

The room was empty – empty of people, that is: the table was full of discarded formal wear, and a smattering of costumes that had apparently been tried on but then passed over in favor of other choices.

As Artie bent down to claim his shoes, his nostrils twitched in delight. He was startled at first, but as he inhaled deeply, he reasoned it out: Mariel, Elyse, Lila, Nanette, and Midge had all been sitting or lying in the nude on this rug, their bodies warm with champagne and romance. So, really, it was no wonder that an overwhelming, delicious aroma of vagina wafted up at him now. *Essence of pussy*, a composite scent built from what each woman had individually contributed, what a vintner would call a *blend*.

"Well, I'll be a monkey's uncle," he muttered in olfactory ecstasy.

"No, there's no time," said Mariel distractedly from across the room. "We need to round up Mickey and find ourselves a cab." Mickey, she informed him, had last been seen roaming the halls dressed as a woodsman – an ordinary nonstannic woodsman, she clarified, as Henry's selection of costumes had not hinted at any forthcoming talkie remakes of *The Wizard of Oz* here in Culver City.

As they hurried into the corridor to undertake these tasks, Artie, still a little high from grape and grope – and now from pan-feminine perfume, too – had a nagging sense that he'd forgotten something.

# Chapter 26

It wasn't until the cast, crew, and staff of *The Sid Heffy Show* had assembled in the studio that Artie discovered, with a shock, what he'd forgotten.

"What the hell are *you* doing here?" Sid bellowed at him. Or rather – so he thought in addressing a man without red hair, glasses, or russet eyebrows – at Mr. Trixton of the Metropolitan Mannequin Company.

"I already have a new sponsor lined up, mister – so if you've come here begging to jump on the Sid Heffy success train, I'm afraid you've missed the boat."

Artie opened his mouth to respond (though he hadn't yet figured out what the appropriate response to this mixed metaphor would be), but Heffy kept talking.

"Anyway, I don't have time to waste on you, Mr. Mannequin Mittens." He looked at the other two erstwhile wedding guests. "You people are late. I need my writers here thirty minutes before a show, dammit. We have changes that need to be made. And where's that new guy, anyway? What's his name ... Placky? Platsky? Pla – "

He stopped cold.

"Hey, wait a minute ..." He was staring straight at Artie, using his most bulbous-eyed, suspicious-vaudevillian gaze.

"You!" he finally said.

Artie froze.

"Yes, *him*," said Mariel Fenton. "And me too, Sid."

"*What?*"

"Artie and I are Metropolitan Mannequins," she said wearily. "Or we used to be – we're out of business now."

Heffy glared at them furiously for a moment. "You're out of business, all right," he finally said in a threatening growl. "But we'll get back to this after the show. Like I said, we need to make some changes in the script."

"What's not working in the script?" Mickey asked solicitously.

"There are a couple of lines I don't understand. You must have done some rewrites after our last session, but I don't get what's going on." He flipped through the typescript. "Like here, for instance, where I say, 'The shutters were flapping in the wind like the flippers on my pet sea lion.' What sea lion? I thought I'm supposed to be a schoolteacher in tonight's play – in a small town in Illinois, right? Suddenly I have a sea lion?"

The writers shifted uncomfortably in their seats.

"And then here's another one," Sid continued. "'Don't you understand that I love you?' I say. 'I've loved you since the first time you made a topsail out of my best checkered trousers and navigated down the M'gongulela.'"

Artie couldn't help smiling with pride as he recalled suggesting that particular river: not only was *Monongahela* a funny word in its correct form, he had argued, but Sid would be sure to mangle it into something even funnier.

Sid was looking at Mickey. "I thought the M'gongulela was in Pittsburgh."

"Oh," said Mickey disingenuously, "is it really? I'm so terrible at geography."

"For chrissake, the script made perfect sense the way it was. Why did you have to fuck around with it? It's almost as if you're trying to get – "

Again Heffy stopped cold. This routine was getting stale, in Artie's opinion.

"*Laughs*," Heffy finished, staring accusingly at Mariel.

The door opened, and the network's Saturday receptionist came in.

"What the hell do *you* want?" barked Heffy.

"I'm sorry to bother you, Mr. Heffy, but Accounting asked me to give you a message. They've been trying to reach your daughter all day ..."

"Yeah, she was at a wedding. So?"

"Would you ask her to call in first thing Monday? Apparently the sponsorship check that Lila Lowell sent for last night's show had the wrong amount on it, and they have to hold it for deposit until that's straightened out."

"*What?*"

"Oh, and the director says two minutes till you're on the air," the secretary added, backing quickly out the door. "Thank you, Mr. Heffy," she finished up melodiously.

# Epilogue

Artie was holding Mariel's hand. "It was awfully generous of you to take responsibility for everything, so Mickey and the others could stay on with Heffy," he said.

They were on the train to Santa Barbara, where Mert's lawyer was waiting with the mannequin-business-dismantling papers.

"It was awfully generous of you, too."

"Yes, but I was only the new guy. This has been your whole world, for so long."

Mariel smiled. "Perhaps it was time for a change. I don't think I realized how tired I was getting of Mr. Sid Heffy."

Artie thought a moment. "Do you really think Sid believed Mickey and company had nothing to do with doctoring the scripts?"

"No, Sid's not *that* stupid. I mean, he's plenty stupid, of course – you will note that it took him four weeks' worth of shows to catch on that there was something funny about the final scripts, so to speak. I was convinced after we slipped the first show by him that he'd *never* notice, which was a big mistake on my part." She paused to take a sip of her Bloody Mary.

"However, recognizing that we were all complicit in the drama-denaturing is an insight that draws on his great gifts for mistrust and suspicion, and Sid is always quick off the mark in that department. But he embraced the illusion of a Mariel-Artie conspiracy because this allowed him to fire only the two of us, instead of his entire staff – which would have been very inconvenient for him, if he did it for keeps."

"I see what you mean. And did you notice that he was so focused on giving us the bum's rush, he seemed to quickly forget how Elyse had betrayed him by accepting help from Lila?"

"Indeed I did," Mariel said happily. "Of course, once we told him Elyse was bowing out of radio, his primary emotion in that area was probably relief. As you yourself hinted when you made your little list, Sid probably didn't remain comfortable for very long with that 'radio dynasty' angle Mickey sold him. He's just too competitive."

Once again, Artie was struck by her wisdom. "Do you think Heffy will give up drama for good now?"

"You know, I think he will. He's tried it twice, and twice it's been a nonstarter. His public wants him to do comedy. His writers want him to do comedy. His new sponsor – providing it's not another Lentilla Dressinger – will certainly want him to do comedy. So, yes, I bet he's ready to go along with all of them, after everything that's happened. Unfortunately – or fortunately – you and I don't get to stick around the swimming pool and see."

They were quiet for a few minutes.

"Artie?"

"Yes?"

"How much influence do you have with Trixie and the gang back home?"

Her words took him by surprise. "You want to go to New York?"

"Well, Lila and Nanette are moving there. And Henry and Midge. So why not Mariel and Artie?" She snuggled into the crook of his arm.

"Damn, if that's how you feel ... then absolutely – why not?"

"Besides, you and I have important things to do in New York."

"We do? What things?"

"I haven't quite thought of them yet. But I'm open to suggestions."

He smiled. "If only Elyse were going too, then we could make a full party of it."

"Oh, I have a feeling that Elyse Heffernan, rising goddess of the stage, will soon be visiting Broadway on a regular basis."

He nodded. "I have a feeling you're right."

"And when she does, it will be up to you and me, kid – well, you and me and the rest of New York – to give her all the sex and laughter she'll be craving while she's away from her pool and Sid's comedy writers."

They kissed.

"Next stop, Santa Barbara!" said the conductor.

That reminded Artie of something. "Hey, what about Sheridan? Aren't you going to miss those special ass-rubs?"

Her salacious smirk went right to his groin. "I thought I'd arrange for you to take a correspondence course."

"I *see*," said Artie with interest.

"Mind you, I doubt you'll really need it ... but won't it be fun doing the homework!"

# About the Author

Jeremy Edwards, described by the Erotica Readers & Writers Association as "one of the most original and amusing erotic authors around," is the author of the erotocomedic novels *Rock My Socks Off* (Xcite Books) and *The Pleasure Dial* (1001 Nights Press), and the erotic-story collection *Spark My Moment* (Xcite). His quirky, sensuous tales have appeared in over fifty anthologies with numerous publishers large and small, including four volumes in the *Mammoth Book of Best New Erotica* series, and he has contributed scores of short stories to print and online magazines.

As a guest on the Web circuit, Jeremy has been seen or heard at Erotica Readers & Writers Association, Erotica for All, LiberatorOoh, LoveHoney, 4-Letter Words, Lust Bites, How to Write Erotic Fiction, Dr. Dick's Sex Advice, Sexy Librarian, Vibe Erotic Book Club, Air Atta Ca Talk, Oh Get a Grip! F-Stop, Rachel Kramer Bussel Online Book Club, and Cult of Gracie Radio. In the nonvirtual world, he has appeared at In the Flesh, Essensuality, and Ravenous Nights in New York, the Erotic Literary Salon in Philadelphia, In the Flesh: L.A. (via telephone), the Seattle Erotic Art Festival (showcase display), and Arts Night Out Northampton (Massachusetts); and as the host of Sexy Scribes Speaking (in Turners Falls, Mass.).

Jeremy's work explores sex in its sunniest form, celebrating joyful sensuality, libidinous urgency, offbeat romanticism, and the pleasures of language and laughter—with the focus on cerebral, sexually self-aware women (some of whom take greater than average pleasure in peeing), and the men and women who adore them. Readers can drop in on him unannounced (and thereby catch him in his underwear) at www.jeremyedwardserotica.com.